I/S 041,042

£6-95,

205

The Love Siege

Also by Tom Wakefield:

Trixie Trash, Star Ascending
Special School
Some Mothers I Know
Isobel Quirk in Orbit

The Love Siege

Tom Wakefield

Routledge & Kegan Paul
London and Henley

First published in 1979
by Routledge & Kegan Paul Ltd
39 Store Street,
London WC1E 7DD and
Broadway House,
Newtown Road,
Henley-on-Thames,
Oxon RG9 1EN
Set in Baskerville 11/13pt by
Hope Services, Abingdon
and printed in Great Britain by
Lowe & Brydone Ltd
Thetford, Norfolk

British Library Cataloguing in Publication Data

Wakefield, Tom

The love siege.
I. Title
823'.9'1F   PR6073.A37/

ISBN 0 7100 0221 1

For
Clare Palmer,
Philippa Brewster
and
Norman Franklin

'But were some child of yours alive at that time,
You should live twice — in it and in my rhyme.'

'Sonnets' – William Shakespeare

1

Mrs Marjorie Prentice took a gentle sip of tea from the thick lip of the cheap mug as though it were of bone china. Her mouth creased a centimetre at each corner, denoting the beginnings of a smile that would never dawn.

'We seem to have got through quite a lot this evening, I feel quite dizzy with all that we have been hearing about. Things we have done, things we are going to do, and things that we might do.' She sighed.

'I'm sorry I feel I have to bring up a matter under AOB.' Her nose wrinkled as she simpered out an apology as tempered and lethal as a steel razor-blade. The mouth stayed tinged in smile, but the nostrils on her face widened as if AOB were an introduction to some form of rancid smell.

'Item five — Any Other Business,' said Isobel Quirk, headmistress.

It had been a long staff meeting, over an hour and a half.

One or two teachers had glanced at the clock and one of the oldest members of staff had begun to nod his head a little and half-close his eyes. In spite of the pressures of the outside world the staff of eight remained behind to talk about the wounded lives of the children in their daily care. In some cases it helped them forget their own wounds a little, so they were not being entirely selfless. Mrs Isobel Quirk did not feel the need to interpret the reasons why people chose or needed to care for others. She was not nor had ever claimed to be a psychiatrist. Nevertheless, Mrs Prentice did confound this charitability of outlook so Isobel chose to be bewildered by her — it was the only way that she could remain constantly fair to the woman. Isobel never placed a great deal of investment on personal loyalty and yet time and time again Mrs Prentice had conceded what she termed 'principles' out of personal loyalty for her headmistress. Loyalty had certainly not been the factor that had bound together the eight teachers who had been with her these ten years since the opening of the school. It was most extraordinary that there were no staff changes in a school of this nature. The local educational directors, and it was rumoured even sections of the national government, were highly suspicious of the situation.

Meetings of a political nature were, in 1983, forbidden by the government, which had been swept to power on a wave of public disenchantment with other political parties, and under new statutory laws all school staff meetings were obliged to have an officer of the government in attendance. Known as parochial guardians they were to report back to the central authorities anything which might be subversive. So some schools held two staff meetings. The official one attended by the parochial guardian was a minute by minute account of what each teacher taught. The unofficial one dealt with all the tapestry of caring and distress that most schools contain. In this sense the planned but clandestine meeting was what the school was all about. In the absence of the guardian the staff felt they could be truthful. The commodity

2

— truth — was a luxury in the present state of purge and enforced conformity by the government.

Mrs Prentice placed her empty mug of tea on the table in front of her with such care one might have thought it some priceless *objet d'art*. For a few seconds she scrutinised the dregs and then slowly raised her head.

'What I have to say is — er — of a delicate nature.' She gave Isobel an appealing but watery-eyed smile. 'I would have preferred a word in your ear first, it might have avoided any undue contention that may arise.'

'Now we're for it,' thought Isobel.

'I shouldn't worry about being contentious, Marjorie, it's healthy for all of us,' said Isobel, clearing her head to cope with any of Marjorie's subtle and clever, divisive contributions.

'Well, I'm really speaking up for dear Miss Bontil.'

Pauline Bontil sat up, suddenly aware. No one had ever spoken up for her before. She unbuttoned the top of her cardigan and sat erect, eager to hear how or in what manner she had been wronged.

'I'm sorry, Pauline, I hadn't realised you were upset about anything,' said Isobel.

Neither had Pauline. So both women were interested in what Marjorie Prentice had to say.

'Far be it from me to say that any child in this school should not be here, but I do feel that if life or limb is at risk, then we should consider excluding the culprit for the corporate good of us all.'

Marjorie paused. Isobel decided to wait for more details and glanced towards Pauline who was clearly puzzled by the formulation of Mrs Prentice's theorem.

Leslie Murt opened wide both of his half-closed eyes; he had been on the verge of sleep and the meanderings of his mind were now called to a halt. He had one year more at school after which, if he chose, he could retire. He was very happy with Isobel Quirk, more happy than she was probably aware of. He did not like or dislike Marjorie Prentice. She was a good teacher and accountable in all duties concerned with the productive running of the school. He pressed a heap of tobacco firmly into his pipe and inhaled deeply, carefully. He distrusted Marjorie Prentice. Her mischievousness was always veiled in goodwill; it was impossible to identify. He puffed and listened; this was no time for a cat-nap even for a tired, ageing deputy-head.

'I really don't know how Miss Bontil can stand it day after day.' Marjorie smiled in Pauline's direction, contrived compassion oozed from every pore. Pauline received the abstract appraisal with suitable humility by lowering her head. Marjorie continued with the glucose treatment. 'How many times were you kicked by him this week, my dear?'

'Oh, just three, no, four times, no more than usual.' Pauline knew who Marjorie was referring to. Barry Narcus was a very difficult child. As though to add to her new role of heroine, Pauline Bontil threw in another minor fact for good measure. 'He bit me on Tuesday afternoon. On the wrist.' She rubbed the injured section. 'There's no trace of a mark now though; I had forgotten the matter.' However, she was enjoying being reminded of it and Marjorie Prentice had more fodder ready.

'Without wishing to make a meal of the situation ...' Mrs Prentice paused to titter a little, 'Oh dear, what an unfortunate metaphor.'

'Clever wicked bitch,' Leslie Murt thought; he puffed at his pipe.

'No, quite seriously, and I really think that this matter is serious, Miss Bontil could have been seriously injured or even killed by such an occurrence.'

'She hasn't described it yet.' Shirley Merchant stopped knitting and placed the half-completed garment on the floor beside her. Mrs Prentice ignored the practical interjection; she usually ignored Shirley, a prickly lady if ever there was one. Shirley had earned a reputation for being 'difficult' yet she was not disliked. This puzzled Mrs Prentice who had failed to

4

muster up any resentment against a teacher who was often both abrasive and rude to her colleagues.

'What sort of situation would we all be in if the bite had gone deeper? What if a vein or an artery had been severed? These are all conjectures, but think of Miss Bontil if — and I say if — Miss Bontil had received such an injury. It would hardly be a laughing matter. I reproach myself for not bringing this matter up sooner.'

'I shouldn't put blame on yourself, Mrs Prentice. After all you have only just found out about the matter, so how could you have mentioned it any earlier?'

The speaker's observation was enhanced by the innocence of its delivery. Miss Margaret Davis never appeared anxious and was an expert at dispersing anxiety from both children and adults. She opened her mouth to continue but Mrs Prentice managed to thwart her.

'Thank you, Margaret dear, for making my position more comfortable. I don't want to hurt anyone's feelings, not even my own. I do feel better now as I would hate to think that you were all thinking that I was attempting to be judgmental on my own behalf. What I have to say does concern all of us and I would like to make it clear that my opinion is proffered in goodwill. I am grateful, Margaret.'

Isobel sat and listened, she could not help but admire the tactics.

'I know the school has a remarkable record for absorbing the flotsam and jetsam of the human condition, but only a fool could accept that Barry Narcus is a piece of plankton that the ocean can easily carry.'

'I don't think any of us imagine that. A child's life is worth more than plankton. But do I understand that you are suggesting exclusion?' Isobel asked. She spoke quickly, it was not necessary to give Marjorie any more broadcasting time.

'Yes, exclusion. I think a case should be made to the guardians for immediate exclusion.'

Marjorie settled back into her armchair. Shirley Merchant

resumed her knitting and Margaret Davis sighed audibly. Leslie Murt seemed to call the meeting back from silence by tapping his pipe on the side of a metal ash-tray.

'Just emptying the debris,' he said.

Everyone knew what exclusion meant for any child who attended a special-care unit in a school for the permanently handicapped, as Isobel's school was now termed. Isobel clasped her hands together and took a quick breath, it was no time to expose her rattled nerve-ends or dogmatise about her feelings which were causing her stomach to somersault. Her outward composure remained bland. Someone else must negate Marjorie's suggestion first, perhaps one or two people, then, she would do a demolition job. She waited, and noticed that Marjorie Prentice glanced out of the window — she was feeling something too. But what?

Isobel would not have forecast that Madge Wragg would be the first counsel for the defence. Madge rarely spoke at staff meetings mainly because she had a constant problem with her dentures. While she was in class she took them out. The children never seemed to notice. By the clever use of lipstick she painted a large cherry-red mouth where the part of her that had been sucked into her throat should have been. It was difficult to describe her face and, with a mixture of cruelty and affection, other members of staff had nicknamed her 'Rainbow'. Her make-up was so thick that no harsh theatre footlights could have penetrated the heavy peach complexion, the rouged cheeks, the kingfisher-blue eyelids, and the perfectly drawn orange eyebrows. Her chestnut-brown hair was quite lovely and always well groomed. It was certainly the most realistic wig that Isobel had ever seen. Very few people were aware that Madge Wragg's hair had once belonged to someone else. Madge gave her upper incisors another shove; the damned things always slipped if she didn't. The older she got the more ill-behaved and mercurial her teeth became. Isobel waited.

'It will mean Section 138 of the Code of Conformity. They'll inject him.' Madge clacked her jaw shut.

'Yes, dear,' said Marjorie scornfully. 'I'm only too painfully aware of that — but we must think of Miss Bontil, and the other children. It is a distressing business.' She glanced out of the window as if the anguish were too much for her.

'She is expecting someone,' thought Isobel.

'It means he will be killed.' Madge spoke softly.

'Oh dear,' murmured Pauline Bontil. Margaret poured Pauline another cup of tea and set it before her. Pauline looked stricken; she would not want to be the instigator of such an event and she felt that she was the instigator. Pauline was not too clever at sorting out how ideas began and what the net result of such ideas might be. Marjorie Prentice was surprised at the extent and depth of Pauline's anxiety. Marjorie Prentice had forgotten that Pauline was a good Catholic. Madge had not.

'You could discuss this issue at confession, not here....'

It was time for Isobel to intervene.

'I'm sure Pauline wouldn't want Barry Narcus killed, and from what information we have as yet received from the guardians, it is certainly not clear that Barry Narcus would come under Section 138, so I feel we need to keep a sense of proportion about both viewpoints offered. One is that Barry Narcus should stay here and two that he should leave us.' Isobel expected an interjection, she expected it from Shirley.

'We don't know whether Section 138 is being enacted or not, the categories are still unclear and the guardian police do have special powers. Since Miss Passmore's forced retirement at Bryantside School, the special-care unit has been dispersed.'

'Dispersed? But where?' Pauline looked genuinely alarmed.

'God knows. The new head was a guardian appointment and she has said nothing. The parents of the children do not know their whereabouts.'

'It could be a relief for some of them. Poor dears, the strain of having such a child about the house must be frightful.'

Marjorie half-yawned and questioned Margaret.

'She's dying of cancer, isn't she?'

'Who?'

'Letitia Passmore.'

'She has cancer, but she is alive. We are all dying slowly in one way or another. It can come at any time, it's not something we choose, is it?'

Margaret's comment was greeted with generalised assent. Marjorie Prentice was quick to sniff defeat; she glanced out of the window again. This time Isobel saw a figure coming down the driveway.

'I don't feel that this issue needs a vote, we all appear agreed that Barry Narcus stays with us.'

'Yes' came from all present. Pauline nodded to add extra intensity to her affirmation. Isobel recognised the figure, it was now less than thirty yards away. She stood.

'I must now quickly inform you that our parochial guardian is almost on top of us.'

'Christ.' Leslie Murt jumped up and bashed more ash from his pipe. Isobel maintained control and fixed him standing where he was with a stare which needed no words. He was ready for orders.

'This meeting is illegal. We must do a Section 138 ourselves and disperse. Leslie, you take Pauline out through the back. You can go out of the gents' lavatory window. For some reason it's bigger than ours. Margaret, you go in the other direction with Shirley and Mr Goldman.'

'You mean the ladies' lavatory window?'

'Yes, you are all thinner, you can scrape through. Do you think your hips are too wide, Reuben?'

'My hips will go through the window.' Reuben Goldman blinked from behind his thick spectacles and pursed his thick large lips. 'It is part of the heritage of a Jewish bachelor to accommodate such situations, he may never know when they will arise.'

The teachers moved and yet still four were left. Beryl Cranford, vegetarian, Christian Socialist, teacher of art and craft, came to her own rescue.

8

'I am going to the medical room to lie down — I have severe stomach cramps. I always do when my periods start. Men cannot bear to hear such details. If Mr Ostanley, our guardian, wants more details he can enquire.' She left.

Madge Wragg had made her way to the door, she called over her shoulder: 'I'll leave naturally from the front entrance. Just a diligent teacher working late. I'll stall him for a bit.'

Isobel was left sitting face to face with Marjorie Prentice.

'I'll just have to go to my classroom, I could be doing work-cards when he arrives. Mr Ostanley is quite interested in the work we do,' Marjorie tittered. 'I can be the one left here on purely legitimate terms.'

'No,' said Isobel.

'Pardon me?'

'No, there will be two of us, Marjorie. I am interested in seeing your work-cards. Mr Ostanley can view us together, we'll both be legitimate. Come, my dear, I am truly interested....' Isobel breathed deeply as she escorted the wasp, who was attempting to sting the life-beat out of her heart, to the classroom.

2

There was not a single bottle of wine in the cellar of the large mansion in Bayswater. Nor did any damp exist. This was just as well, as the whitewashed walls served as a background to what looked like a storage section of the grocery department of some enormous city store. Perhaps there was more order than one would find in a store, perhaps more detail. Seven long, low-ceilinged rooms were all linked to one another by a stone archway. The entrances were without doors and would have been perfectly designed for some place of worship. The straight-backed, white-haired man, dressed in a black jacket and trousers shiny with age, took careful stock of the contents as he drifted from chapel into mosque into temple whichever way his imagination inclined. He ticked off his inventory with meticulous care and deliberation. The tins and their labels were beautiful in his eyes.

Room 1 Protein: corned beef, pilchards, Spam, ravioli,

Margaret's voice appeased his fears and he remained stooping and placed his finger inside the circle once more. He shouted up to her.

'I'm down here. Down here checkin' the stores. Marigold is asleep. It's nearly eight o'clock, I have fed her, and told her a story.'

Margaret slung her coat over the back of one of the two brass herons which stood in the hallway and Shirley clothed the other one in similar fashion.

'Give me your jacket, Reuben. Thank you.'

Margaret balanced his anorak over her heron's tail.

'There.' she said.

'Harry won't be long. Don't worry, everything will be all right.'

'Yes, it will'. Shirley kicked off her shoes; she tended to be a trifle slatternly at home. Harry Wintner had observed this, but he was not upset by it. Reuben watched one of the shoes slither along and crack itself against the wall. He still felt apprehensive.

'It won't shit on your raincoat, Reuben. If it did it would produce a lead ball or even a brass one. It wouldn't stain it. Imagine those creatures shitting brass ball-bearings....'

Shirley's banter did not break Reuben's inhibitions but he managed to grin a little before the two women led him towards the sitting-room. The herons remained unmoved. Margaret introduced the two men.

'Reuben Goldman, meet my common-law father, Harry Wintner.'

The two men shook hands limply. Both were competing as to which of them could be the most awkward and shy.

'Reuben has decided to join us.' Shirley showed them all into the sitting-room as Margaret delivered the information to Harry. The two men scrutinised one another for the first time. They had little option. Shirley had set them down in two high-backed armchairs which faced one another. Without any exchange, Margaret and Shirley left any attempts at

12

scaling the plateau of shyness that both men were prone to be isolated upon. The men must sort it out for themselves. Shirley took some knitting from her bag and clicked furiously. Margaret spread an assorted array of coloured felt-tip pens before her as she sat on the floor. She then commenced decorating and naming an endless supply of work-cards for the forthcoming weeks of school hours.

Both men sat as though they were sitting in the hairdressers. Reuben crossed his legs. Harry noticed that his dark-green socks exactly matched the shade of his polo-necked pullover. Reuben's sop to the aesthetic demands of being clothed ended here. A blue pin-striped suit completed his ensemble. On his identity form next to his identity number was written: complexion sallow, eyes dark brown, nose aquiline, hair thick/coarse/black. Harry thought his complexion almost reflected the green of his pullover. His eyes appeared larger because of the dark shadows beneath them. The glasses, thick rimmed, drew attention to his eyes which was as well as Reuben had been blessed with large undefined lips which seemed ever-wet. He had a nervous habit of licking them. Harry Wintner coughed.

'Ahem.'

'Thank God one of them is going to say something.' Shirley determinedly counted the stitches on one of her knitting-needles and did not look up.

'Ahem, Marigold is asleep. She doesn't like the new head teacher. She was crying when I collected her this afternoon. It's most unusual, she always smiles.'

Harry was addressing Margaret. She placed the purple felt-tip pen on the card before her and looked in his direction.

'Marigold?' Reuben asked.

'Our child,' said Harry.

'Oh, I see,' said Reuben, not seeing or comprehending at all.

'Don't tell lies, Reuben.' Margaret got up from the floor and stood behind Harry's chair. She laid her arm across the top of it, her wrist revealing at least four bangles and bracelets together with the commencement of a tattoo. Reuben had seen the tattoo before. It was a palm-tree. Marjorie Prentice thought it vulgar and Reuben quietly agreed with Marjorie's assessment. Margaret liked her tattoo and invented endless stories surrounding its origin when the children at school asked about.. 'You know you don't see,' she waved her arm and the bangles clattered.

'No, I don't. I don't,' Reuben laughed.

'My common-law mother died when Marigold was born. I adopted my parents. So you see the child is now as much my responsibility as Harry's.'

'When she died they said, "You have a daughter, sir".' Harry Wintner's voice was flat. 'They said, "I'm afraid that your daughter is a mongol". "It's a marigold as far as I'm concerned," I said, "and nobody should be afraid of a marigold." That's our daughter's name — Marigold.'

'Quite right, too,' said Reuben with much conviction.

Margaret went back to her felt-tips.

'I am Jewish you know.' Reuben licked his lips.

'I can see that,' said Harry.

'Ah, but I'm a bachelor.' Reuben threw his words out expecting a ripple to come from the stiff, awkward, elderly man sitting opposite.

'So am I, I have remained so all my life. But I have had my moments so to speak.' Harry closed his eyes and opened them abruptly.

'Yes, some very good moments. And you?'

'The moments might have been, but they have escaped me,' said Reuben sadly. He added. 'I'm forty-two years of age.'

'Your age is no concern of mine. So you have decided to join us here? What about your belongings?'

'One suitcase in the hall. I possess very little.'

'That's good,' said Harry. He continued but rose from his chair and looked out from the window as he spoke.

14

'If things get worse, and most of us here believe that they will, we have decided to stay together and protect and resist.'

'Resist?' Reuben's tongue relished both lips as if they were lollipops.

'Yes, resist. The more there are of us, the easier it will be. This is a large house with good-sized grounds.'

'You make it sound like a pending state of siege. Do you think it might come to that?'

'Yes, I do. Fortunately Sir Vivien Bland who left this house to Margaret and me thought likewise and he had been making slow but adequate preparations for years. Margaret, Shirley and Isobel have continued these preparations with more alacrity over the past eighteen months.' He still looked out on the grounds.

'Isobel?'

'She is here with us, one of us,' said Shirley.

'Good God,' exclaimed Reuben.

'Reuben, please don't blaspheme. Can you pass me the orange felt-tip, it's rolled near your foot? Thanks,' said Margaret, seemingly undeterred from her work by the course of the conversation.

'Come,' Harry Wintner turned from the window. 'I'll show you the cellar.'

Reuben followed him.

Shirley began to clean her finger-nails with one of the knitting-needles. She had cast off and the needle was spare. Margaret paused and watched her digging the needle-point between her finger-nails. If this wasn't enough, Shirley had more to follow. She wiped the grime from the needle on her skirt and then began to poke about her left ear with the instrument. A few bits of wax were inspected and some had fallen on her shoulder. She fingered the edge of the needle clean, ready to start another probe. Margaret was about to remonstrate with her when they heard the calls from below. They were urgent calls. Neither of the men were given to excessive exchanges. The women left their preoccupations and descended the stone stairway as quickly as they possibly could. The cellar was lit up.

'We are in here — the last one,' Harry hooted. 'Come, come, come quickly. Reuben is marvellous, marvellous.' The word echoed and guided them into the last chamber of the cellar. The two men knelt at the far edge of the dark circle.

'Stop'. Harry Wintner held up a pickaxe as though he were some incanting ancient Druid.

Reuben showed them the palm of his hand as if he were directing traffic. 'Don't walk across the circle, come round. Come, come.'

Margaret had rarely seen Harry in such a state of agitation or euphoria. The women knelt down beside the two men. A small hole had been hacked out of the concrete immediately in front of them. Harry picked up a fragment of stone. He held it a few inches from the hole, then dropped it.

'Shush, listen.'

The plopping sound was quite distinct. Quite clear.

'We have a well beneath the house. We have our own water-supply.'

Reuben rubbed his hands together as a gleeful child might. He took the pickaxe from Harry and chipped further along the concrete. 'See, see, it falls away quickly, we could have the well in operation with less than a day's work between us.'

'How did you know that it was a well?' Shirley dropped a bigger chunk of concrete down. The splash was more distinct.

'It could only have been a well, what else could it have been?'

'I think we should pray,' said Margaret.

'Don't be so medieval,' Shirley snapped and snatched the pickaxe from Reuben and began to hack at a piece of concrete. A piece flew from the ground and struck Reuben at the side of the head. He took off his spectacles.

'God, oh God, I'm sorry,' she said.

Reuben stood and adjusted his glasses. 'They're not broken. but Margaret is quite right.'

16

'About what?' asked Shirley who was inspecting the side of his head for any trace of injury.

'About … about,' he paused. 'I think we should go upstairs now.'

Harry led the way. They waited in the next chamber for Margaret to join them. Even Shirley did not wish to call her from the edge of the well. They watched her rise and saw her smile. This smile passed from her to them. It stated that they were corporate and they all found it most satisfying. She joined them in the armament room.

'You should stack the Luger pistols elsewhere, keep the Brens and Berettas on the other side. The grenades ought to be over here too, nearer the detonators. There's no reason why they shouldn't be labelled alphabetically like the rest of the supplies.' Reuben spoke rapidly but with authority.

'How do you know about such things?' Shirley viewed Reuben with a new-found awe. She had only ever seen him sucking and blowing on a recorder and had rarely spoken to him. He never talked much at school, but then, for that matter, neither did she.

'I read and I make music,' he replied.

'We will eat now. I think your suggestions are wise, Reuben.' Harry led them upstairs as he voiced his opinions.

It was a wholesome meal; Harry was an excellent cook. Some stew was set aside for Isobel who had not yet returned. It was now eight-thirty.

'I'll show you your room — you have it to yourself for now, but at a later date it might be necessary for you to share. I hope you won't mind.' Harry had brought Reuben's suitcase into the sitting-room.

'Wragg said she'd be here by nine-thirty. She is joining us too.' Margaret spoke to all the company then to Reuben directly.

'She will share with you, Shirley,' Harry added.

'No she will not,' said Shirley decisively.

'But —'

Shirley cut in on Harry. 'I'm fond of Madge, but I can't share a room with her. Put Reuben's bag in my room. Don't look alarmed, Reuben, it's a large room with two beds. I won't attack you.'

Reuben looked discomfited by the arrangement but nodded his head as Harry indicated him to follow.

'Shirley, you could have frightened him away.' Margaret began to stack the food bowls on top of one another.

'I don't think so. What's more I'm going to have him.'

'Shirley — please — keep your voice down, he might hear you.'

'All right, all right,' Shirley whispered. 'But I am going to have him. I have decided. I am intent on having him.' She brushed aside the thin, straggly fringe of hair from her eyes. 'In the meantime, I'll help you with the washing up.'

3

Madge Wragg squeezed past the walnut sideboard which stood in the hallway of her small semi-detached house in Neasden. There were only three houses left in the street as the rest had been demolished and Madge's own house had been condemned for execution under what was called a Compulsory Purchase Age State Requirement Order. Madge winced as she hit her shin-bone against a drawer protruding from the sideboard. She slammed the drawer shut. The lady from the central State offices for the aged had called three weeks previously.

'At sixty-eight, dear, it's time for you to be resting. I can't see how it is that you are still working. They must have made a special case out for you on that count. I am afraid that I am in no position to make such allowances and I think that a little later you will see that what we have decided is for your own good.'

Madge had sulked and not answered the wretchedly smart-looking young woman with the short, healthy, cropped hair. She would have liked to have said that she would prefer to decide what was good for her, herself. And what did the woman mean by 'the long run'? If she was talking about living, then Madge thought she was a fool as she intended to go on living how she felt. She did not feel sixty-eight. On her good days she looked only fifty and on her bad days even when she was ready for bed, she might look tired, but not old; no, not elderly. The woman had said that there was far too much furniture in the house. This was true. Madge had been married three times and one tended to collect things. It was difficult to discard. Now she was expected to select and move into a one-bedroom flat on an estate for the elderly. Madge snorted with disdain as she made her way into her bedroom. There was even a matron hovering around the place in a black and red uniform. Madge sat in front of her dressing-table mirror and removed the rings from her fingers. She stroked her creased throat.

'No vampire is going to watch over me,' she grinned at herself in the mirror.

A strict routine was adhered to three times each day in this position. Today was different. The routine had to be changed. She had a journey in the offing. First she took off her hair. A lovely chestnut creation. She gave it a good shake and brushed it carefully before placing it on the top of an up-turned goldfish bowl. Her teeth were plopped into a tumbler of water with a mouth-hygiene tablet that fizzed them clean. She slopped a great puddle of pink sticky lotion into the palm of her hand, rubbed it with the fingers of her other hand and applied the stuff in generous fashion all over her face. Watching her face dissolve before her very eyes in this way caused her no dismay. In fact, she quite enjoyed the operation. It was like painting her own picture. The beauty of it all was that one could make slight adjustments or improvements twice a day and in this way one was an ever-changing work of art. She was sure that some people appreciated it. The children did. Mrs Quirk did. So damn the woman from the State offices. A little powder on *her* nose wouldn't do her any harm. Or? Madge blinked and cackled. Or, up her rotten nose. She wiped away the lotion with wodges of cotton wool and erased her face. No water had touched it for years.

Thin grey wisps of hair floated here and there over islands of baldness. The hair had begun to fall out not long after she married her second husband. It was diagnosed as alopecia. The growth never really recovered — but she did. The third husband was the best of the bunch. He had encouraged her to 'fan-dyke up' as he called it. Then when his illness came with the colostomy bag, she expected him to change; but no, he was as attentive as ever and even more stuff went on. He liked it, he loved her to look bright. Three days before his death they had made love (of a kind) and nothing, not even his appalling illness, had revolted her.

She allowed one tear before preparing her facial base. She began from the top and completed her eyebrows and eyelids. Then she heard the knock at the door. She placed a towel over her head so she could quickly draw it across her face if needs be.

'Who is it?' she cooeed through the letter-box.

'It's me. Mrs Quirk. Isobel Quirk.'

Madge called back. 'I'm only a quarter ready dear. Just a quarter of me is ready.'

'I cannot wait on the doorstep, Madge.'

Madge recognised a trace of irritability in Isobel's tone and gingerly let her into the hallway, slamming the door shut behind her before she was barely in the house.

'Squeeze yourself in, dear. I'm sorry, I thought you might have been that vampire who is trying to put me on the first step to an old folks' home. Trying to put me on sticks before I am ready. Well, I'm not ready. And when I am, she'll not get within a mile of me.'

Isobel could not take her eyes from Madge who looked as though she were ready for a masked ball. Her eyes glittered, but her mouth and hair barely existed. Madge pushed open the door immediately on Isobel's left.

'Wait in the front room — just give me another half-hour and I'll be ready.'

'Half an hour?' Isobel could not hide the exasperation. She was tired.

'Well, twenty minutes then.'

Madge scooted upstairs and Isobel settled herself in an armchair which was jammed between an old-fashioned radiogram and an obsolete television set. Indeed, the room was so full of furniture that she felt quite overpowered by it all; she felt as though she had been plonked in the middle of an auction room. She called upstairs to Madge.

'I'll make some tea, Madge. I'll feel my own way round the kitchen.'

Madge did not answer. Isobel made her way to the kitchen, Madge had not negated her request. It was likely that she was organising her mouth so she couldn't speak anyway. Somehow, Isobel managed to find two cups and the tea was ready when Madge descended.

'There,' said Madge announcing herself like the clown in a Shakespearean play. 'I couldn't answer when you called, I was working on my face.'

'I guessed as much,' Isobel replied flatly.

She watched Madge suck in her tea. A cyclamen semi-circle spangled with silver was left on the lip of the cup. Madge had really gone haywire with the lipstick this time. Madge's eyes stared from their deep prune-like sockets. Madge interpreted Isobel's distaste as wonder.

'Isn't it a marvellous colour? "November camellia", that's what the shade is. You do like it?'

'They don't grow, I mean camellias don't flower, in November.'

'That's just the point, Isobel dear, if they did then they might be flecked with snow, hence the silver splatterings. The children love it.'

Isobel did not, but showed compassion merely by changing the subject.

'Are all your things in the one trunk? What arrangements have you made about the house?'

'All I need is in the trunk. Yes.'

Madge poured herself some more tea and twirled her cup around in the saucer. She's intent on leaving another transfer behind thought Isobel. Madge continued.

'As for the house, well, what can I say? The bulldozers will be along in two months time so there is no sense of loss there. After all, it's only been a place of shelter these past five years. Just shelter. I would have been quite as happy living in a large sewage pipe. You know, like the ones we used to see pictures of poor Indian families living in — back in the good old days when posters weren't monitored.'

'The furniture, there seems to be a great deal of —'

'Oh, they can do what they like with it, I have no affection or affiliation for inanimate things. All these bits and pieces seemed useful at the time they were bought, but now they seem silly. Most purchasing is. All that matters is how you look and how you are. Do I pass my own test?' Madge trilled coyly.

Isobel smiled.

'Yes, Madge, you do.'

'You haven't had another form have you — about my age?'

'I lied by seven years.'

'Good girl, they'll catch up on you, though, some time.'

'I think that they are catching up already, Madge.'

Isobel rested her head in both hands unable to repress the fatigued sigh. She gritted her teeth and kept them clenched shut as she spoke.

'Our parochial guardian, Mr Ostanley, scrutinised our roll. He had a check-list on genetic disorders and what he termed as "children alien to the needs of the State". He asked me if mongols could ever be truly integrated into the glorious scheme of things to be. I said it was dependent on the scheme.

He accused me of being evasive. He showed me a list of our special-care children. He had made no comment about them — but a green line had been ruled, neatly, very neatly, through all their names. They were erased as far as he was concerned. He said that Section 138 would soon be implemented and asked for my comments. I had none. Then he gave me this.'

Isobel took a small yellow card from her bag. The card had letters and numbers on it. Stamped over the small print was her name. Madge took the card. She held it at some distance from her eyes; she would never admit to being long-sighted consequently, she had to read everything as though she were viewing through a telescope.

'What does it mean?'

'It's what is termed a preliminary caution. He was very polite about it all, formal and polite. Yet, he indicated very clearly that if I were to receive a blue card — which is next in line — I could be held in custody for an unlimited period pending analysis of ideals and definitions. I felt like one of the flats or houses that he sells; he wanted to know my contents and every recess. Madge, I am afraid that I have been catalogued.'

'You're like my house, then.'

'Yes, I'm due for demolition.'

'And the special-care children?'

'Yes, those too.' Isobel ran her fingers through her short-cropped hair and threw back her head.

'You can't be demolished before you are ready. I should know that. My dear, I'm an expert on restoration. I have been at it for the last ten years. We are prepared. Anxiety is quite useless, most of us are with you. Aren't we? Look, I have a half-bottle of port, let's finish it off.' Madge hauled the bottle from underneath the tea-cosy. 'It's room temperature, just right. The only way to deal with really horrid matters is to celebrate them, or celebrate confounding them.'

Isobel downed a glass and had it quickly replenished. The alcohol made her flush and slashed some of her usual restraint.

'Confound? Yes we must confound them. At present, Margaret, Shirley, Reuben, you and myself are committed. As you know, I left Margaret to do all the approach work.'

'Yes, she's good at it.'

'She is seeing Beryl next week; I'm not sure about Pauline and it just wouldn't be fair to ask anything of Leslie.'

'I think it would be rotten unfair if you didn't. He'd be most grievously hurt if he found out that he was excluded from the plan. He will find out eventually, he will have to.' Madge pouted to please the mirror hanging behind Isobel's head. Then looked back to Isobel. 'I think you are being most unfair to Leslie, he would leap like a labrador if you gave him the chance.'

'I was thinking of his wife, Madge.'

'So was I. See that Margaret has him with us by next week. Pauline? I don't know either. Margaret can sort that out.'

'There's just Marjorie Prentice left.'

'She should be dead,' said Madge.

Isobel thought of Marjorie; she had barely left the woman an hour ago. Marjorie Prentice had actually kissed her on the cheek. Was it the left or the right?

'You go right on home, dear, you look all in, don't worry about the record books. Now off you go and get a good rest tonight, you can push yourself too far. None of us here would like that and I'm not going to let you over-tire yourself. I will see the school-keeper locks up if Mr Ostanley chooses to stay and look around a little longer.' She had entered Isobel's room and apologised for not knocking after Mr Ostanley had given Isobel the yellow card. 'Oh, I'm sorry, my dear, I'd thought that you were alone in the eyrie. It's so difficult to get hold of you during the day.'

Her lies were told with such authority that one had to be convinced that she believed them herself.

Out-manoeuvred, Isobel had left the two of them together, receiving their sympathy as it was intended — like henbane diluted with the tiniest spottle of wine. At least Isobel was in no doubt that Marjorie was in collusion with Guardian Ostanley. She had been warned, but had chosen not to take heed of the warnings; now she had little alternative.

'Oh, dear God,' said Isobel in half-prayer, not blasphemy.

'What's wrong? Have you forgotten something?' asked Madge draining the last of the port.

'Yes, Beryl. Beryl Cranford. She was still in the medical room when I left.'

Isobel was worried. Madge was ready; it was getting dark and she was curious to see her new home and wanted to see herself out of Neasden.

'If you take the front of the trunk, I'll take the back. They always used to be carrying them when we used to have pantomimes.'

The two women staggered to Isobel's car and placed the trunk in the boot. Madge took her house keys from her pocket and dropped them down a drain conveniently situated in the nearby gutter.

'Do you remember pantos, Isobel?'

'Just, yes, just,' said Isobel as the engine revved.

No one quite knew what had happened to the architect who had originally designed the school building. When Isobel first saw it she was more than pleasantly surprised, perhaps overjoyed. Before she had seen the building she had heard muttered complaints from administrators who were stricken by the strange demands being made for building materials and the unusually high number of carpenters who were difficult to come by. She had heard the clerk of the works groan and whine and refer to the building as something straight out of Grimms' *Fairy Tales*.

'Bloody grim, that's what it is, bloody grim.'

The plans and building of the school had provided him with headaches too and he was eternally bitter about its eventual birth. Nevertheless, it was built and now stood strident in its non-conformity.

Apart from the walls, which were of grey breeze block, the

27

building was entirely made up of wood, glass and eight perspex domes. There was a central hall surrounded by what looked like eight beehives. These mounds rose like mosque domes from a wooden-beamed roof-top covered by a weird mixture of straw and plaster. 'It's biblical,' thought Isobel.

There was a sense of time to the place and initially Isobel felt that if it had rained hard the building might have been washed away. There had been much rain over the years. The building had not been washed away — but the roof did leak in all kinds of odd places. Tower-blocks skirted the school, and gave it a cartoon-like appearance. You could have your choice. Either joke about the building or cherish it. Isobel cherished it daily; there were heating failures and leaks in the tower flats and they had no aesthetic appeal. The school would not have looked out of place in *The Arabian Nights*, the Brothers Grimm would not do. The building did have drawbacks but some of these proved to be undeniably useful.

The hot-water bottle that Beryl Cranford had placed between her legs had gone cold. She had placed it there while she lay in the medical room. It would have authenticated her story if Ostanley had ogled his way into the room. She slung the cold rubber bag from her. There was no point in risking a chill in her fanny for his sake. She heard a strange trickling noise. Alarmed, she jumped off the bed thinking that the hot-water bottle might be leaking its contents. The cap was intact, but the gurgling and bubbling increased and reached a crescendo of geyser-spouting proportions and then began to sigh slowly to a halt. It was the water-pipes emptying themselves for the day. None of the pipes were hidden, they were exposed, indeed defined in different colours, in each room. This had been Isobel's idea. They curled like brightly coloured snakes throughout the building and occasionally gurgled and croaked like marsh frogs or toads. The pipes had stopped their evening chorus and Beryl put them to better purpose than carrying water or heating.

Within a short time the staff had realised that they had an

intercom system inside the school by constructional mistake or default. Beryl placed her ear to the pipe. The voices were resonant and clear; they sounded as if the two people were talking in a cave with a waterfall murmuring in the background yet not impeding chatter. Marjorie Prentice's plum-sounding voice fluted into Beryl's receiver.

'Far be it from me to make observations — but before the National Assembly were elected — er — how can I put it. Er — precocious, yes precocious appointments were made which just could not have happened today. I am afraid, Mr Ostanley, that you have one such inheritance. I feel for you, as I know that you are a sensitive man and that it must be quite a heavy cross for you to bear.'

There was a pause. Beryl could imagine the sorrowful shake of the head, the look of pained bewilderment.

'You have been more than patient. I have said as much to Mrs Quirk myself. She doesn't live with her husband you know. I have heard that she never sees him at all. Quite an errant man by all accounts, but then, she's not the best judge of character. The things she has said about y— Oh dear. I've said too much.'

'About me, Mrs Prentice?'

'I really didn't want to bring it up,' said Marjorie.

'Vomit and bile,' thought Beryl as she pressed her ear closer to the water-pipe.

'I must remind you, Mrs Prentice, that if you choose to withdraw or contain any information which you might consider to be a disservice to the State, you could be placing yourself in an uncomfortable position. I know that you are a most reasonable lady. Now, say what you have to say. Get on with it, woman.'

Ostanley's voice had changed its tone; Beryl felt really sick now. Previous to this all she had seen was a little estate agent and Party member who always took copious notes and left abruptly. So this was what the man was really like. Margaret Davis had always insisted that he was wicked, but could never substantiate her feelings. Beryl, who affiliated Christianity with astrology, had worked out by numbers from his birth sign, his date of birth and the Bible, that he was no good. She half-smiled with satisfaction — wait till Isobel Quirk heard about this. Marjorie Prentice was not too frightened to present her gangrene; gently it flooded the water-pipes. Mr Ostanley had taken out a notebook. Beryl needed no such aid as Mrs Prentice's words scorched and branded her innards.

'Mrs Quirk refers to you as "that man" and the rest of the staff refer to you as a "pluke"?'

'Pluke? What does it mean?'

'I believe that it is a Scottish word, or of Scottish derivation. A pluke is a small festering pimple, most unpleasant.'

'Obscene,' Ostanley rasped.

'I quite agree, only twisted minds could have concocted such a nasty nomenclature. I have never heard Mrs Quirk condemn this kind of reference, by ignoring it she is condoning it. But that snippet of information is only the tip of the iceberg of what goes on in this building. The tip of the iceberg.'

Ostanley then did something to shock Mrs Prentice. Beryl heard her gasp.

'Oh, oh dear.'

Marjorie's voice wobbled. The tremors were clearly genuine.

'In case you are unaware, the card in your hand indicates that you are now under a debt of honour to inform. If you withhold anything you could be held in custody for some time. Now, Mrs Prentice, I am expecting to hear quite a lot from you. None of your gullet-sugared, piss-arsed gossip. Give me something to act on or you could be in jeopardy yourself. A sensible woman like you doesn't want to be caught with her drawers down behind a nettle patch. She might get pushed over, then squatting would never be the same again.'

Marjorie was frightened; she had not known that Ostanley could be so cruel, nor had she considered his power. Malicious gossip she enjoyed, but she had not felt threatened, not ever, by her own measured barbs. Now she had to disgorge all kinds of myths or nastiness and unprofessionalism in order to survive. She was not happy, she was not comfortable. The dampness under her armpits and around her crutch spread further. Oh, how she had misjudged Ostanley. The others were right. She felt trapped, and like some caged bird twittered away what Ostanley required of her, hoping that at some time she would be allowed to stop fluttering and be set free.

'Perhaps I can itemise the points for you. I will call out the shopping list and you present the goods. Don't bugger about either. Just present the goods. Secret meetings?'

'Yes. Numerous, one each week for the past eight months.'

'Would discussion warrant harm to the ideals for national unity? Answer, you cow. Don't turn those big eyes on me. Get your udder working. Would discussion warrant harm to the ideals for national unity?'

'Yes, yes.'

'Do you think that any of the teachers could be classified under the non-integration group? Would you say that any of them were marginals?'

'Yes, all of them.'

'Does that include yourself?'

Ostanley laughed, he was enjoying himself.

'No, no, Mr Ostanley. If it did, I wouldn't be sitting here, would I?'

'I'm asking the questions.' He enjoyed watching Marjorie's terror.

'Any State achievements presented, any State dogmas inculcated?'

'The children here wouldn't understand, they ...,' Marjorie had her defences slashed.

'Just answer.'

'No, no State achievements presented. No State dogmas declared or inculcated.'

She added, 'But there is a lot of love here, a lot of caring, on the whole —'

31

'You should have thought of that before; keep your senti-
mentality for your handbag. Any relationships, sexual relationships, between members of staff?'

'Not that I know of, they all seem quite fond of each
other.'

'No lesbianism or poofter goings-on between them?'

'Oh, no, no.' Marjorie felt ill, frightened sick.

'Think of something that might be going on. Use your
head woman and don't blubber.'

Marjorie had begun to cry. Her head was jerked back as he
struck her cheek. Beryl heard it; a stifled cry followed.

'I think that Leslie Murt is very fond of Mrs Quirk. I think
that he loves her.'

'Has he had her? On or off the premises?'

'Pardon?'

'You heard, on or off the premises. One or the other,
which is it?'

'I'm sure it had never been declared in that fashion. I think
Mrs Quirk is unaware of its existence, I think —'

Ostanley shrieked at her. 'On or off, or both?'

'Off, off the premises,' said Marjorie.

'I think I have enough here to be going on with, quite a
little hornet's nest of one kind or another. You're not excused.'

Marjorie had stood to leave; she sat immediately he spoke.
She felt drained and quite destroyed.

'You will report each day at 4.45 p.m. at the Central Office
of National Inquiry until further notice. You will now be
placed under constant surveillance; you have retained this
information for far too long. And you too are now suspect.
There is a chance that if we glean enough from you that you
may come out of all this lightly. You will discuss this meeting
with no one, that is if you possess any respect.'

'Respect?'

'Respect for your own life, Mrs Prentice. Now good day to
you, I shall inform the school-janitor to lock up. I suggest
that you go straight home.'

Beryl Cranford waited and checked her watch, she had heard the key turn in the door. The medical room had been locked and was not inspected. She was imprisoned for the night. She looked up at the small window and then gazed down at her ample hips. Desperation goaded her into working out any possibility of escape. She must tell Isobel all that she had heard without delay and she was suffering from an internal agony, an urgent need to urinate. The physical demands on her impaired her imagination. This was no time to be thinking of status. She took off all her clothes except her bra, climbed on to the draining board and relieved herself in the sink. It was a delicate operation, but she felt happier and experienced some sense of triumph when she had finished it. She removed her bra. Perhaps naked ... naked. Yes, naked. That was the way out. She surveyed her hips once more. They ballooned out from her as though someone had applied a bicycle pump to her lower half. Nature could be most unfair from time to time.

She foraged through her handbag before finally up-ending it on the floor to see which of her accoutrements might be useful. Hairbrush — no good; powder compact — useless; mirror — she couldn't signal Morse code, the sun had gone down and who could she signal to. Hand cream — hand cream, yes. She squeezed the plastic bottle empty, but its pink-blue sticky content barely covered her left thigh and buttock. She was ready to cede to despair when she noticed the nail-file. She seized it and began to pick at the delicate lock on the medical cupboard, with a great deal of wiggling, cajoling and odd prayer, the cupboard lock gave in and she gazed at the lint, the disinfectant, the tweezers, the plasters, and the rows and rows of bottles of baby lotions which were used for the incontinent children. She took six bottles and fondled them as though she were anticipating a celebration.

'Champagne, for the love of God,' she muttered.

Bottle after bottle of the rather sickly scented lotion was emptied on her; she massaged her neck, her shoulders, her breasts. It was not an unpleasant exercise. Her thighs and bottom were given a thorough soaking, and in a matter of minutes, she stood as slimy and slippery and naked as an eel. She pondered over her heaped belongings but then, shrugging her shoulders, gathered them together and put them near the chair which she had placed beneath the small window. She peered out. No one. Her blouse was used as a make-do hold-all and she tied the arms of the garment round her belongings and packaged them into a neat, pleasant-looking bundle. This was squeezed and pushed through the window; much to Beryl's satisfaction she heard it strike the ground with a dull thud outside.

In her first attempt at hauling herself up to the window-ledge she almost knocked herself out. Having grasped the outside ledge of the window and managing to heave herself up as far as her shoulders the lotion worked too well; her fingers slipped and Beryl cracked her chin on the window-sill as she crashed backwards on the carpet. The blow had dazed her, but it taught her a sharp lesson; she wiped her hands on the carpet until her palms and fingers were bone dry. The second attempt at ascent was successful. She would have preferred to have gone through the window feet first. However, the extra leverage needed would have exhausted her already strained physical resources. She pushed through the window as a buxom female swimmer plunges for the water. She surfaced but hung in mid-air. A sharp stab of pain seemed to come from both sides of her body and Beryl knew that she was stuck.

She bit her bottom lip and, within what her present confines would allow, began to wriggle and squirm. Darts of pain shot into her hip-bone as she flung her torso forward and then sideways. Her body now became wedged sideways — she had progressed a little but was beginning to feel dizzy and sick. The hair-grips had fallen from her hair so that it had uncoiled itself from its usual secure bun and fell in long tresses over her head and shoulders stretching towards the ground.

Beryl had never been caught with her hair down before. She put more effort into her exertions; again the movement forward was only fractional. She cried out in anger and frustration more than sorrow or pain and eventually let herself hang limp and still. She thought of St Peter and hoped.

All that was visible of the two men were their lower halves. Beryl's eyes stared at two sets of oil-stained flies. She blinked; one of the men was fingering the buttons, not avidly, but gently, as though he were in some state of indecision.

Beryl spoke. 'I'm awfully sorry, I seem to have got myself into rather a mess.'

The man took his hand from his fly buttons. 'We can see that, Mrs; you could get yourself arrested, lying like that in your birthday suit.'

'Help me, please help me.' Beryl feigned sobs and tears. 'I'm stuck. I'll explain once I have my feet back on the ground.'

'P'raps we should get the fire brigade or the police.'

'No, no, don't do that, I'm sure that won't be necessary,' she wailed.

'Come on, Arthur, I'll take her shoulders and you try shunting from the middle half. It makes a change from laying rail-tracks. We can change ends for a bit of variety if the going gets rough.'

Both men broke into choking laughter, but even as they did so, Beryl was comforted to feel the coarsened hands grasp certain contours of her body that no man had ever known the geography of before.

'Christ.' The man who had grasped her shoulders pulled, only to find his hands slipping off her. He fell backwards on the ground.

'Better wipe her top part, Len, she's covered in grease. We have to wipe you over, Mrs, OK?'

'Yes, please do, it's most thoughtful of you.' Beryl was in no situation to consider options. She gave them every encouragement.

They seemed to wipe her with excessive thoroughness, her breasts receiving particular care. Nevertheless, she offered no complaint and the men worked at her with a diligence and concentration that would have made the railway company proud.

'Right, we'll try again. You take the shoulders this time, Arthur, and I'll take the middle.'

'I'll be buggered if I will. We'll toss for it.'

'Pardon?' said Beryl who was feeling a little better, quite refreshed in fact.

'Tails; I take the middle.'

Beryl's middle was taken and once more Beryl felt that the hands manoeuvred with undue care. At one point, something happened — it must have been an odd finger or a thumb — which made her jump. This proved helpful as a simultaneous tug at her shoulders brought her flopping out of the window like jelly leaving a mould. The sides of her thighs were badly grazed, but she was complete. Half of her shone and glistened in the moonlight. The men, who were of middle age, stood and awaited her next move. Did they expect a reward?

Hastily she slipped on her blouse and climbed into her skirt, put on her shoes and picked up her handbag. She reached for her purse and proffered a five pound note.

'You have been very kind, I don't know what would have happened to me without your help, please take this. I'm sorry I can't afford more. Your help has been worth more than you could ever possibly realise.'

'No, no, hang on to it,' the men chorused.

'How very kind of them,' thought Beryl as she watched them saunter off into the night. It wasn't until she was speeding by taxi-cab towards the house in Bayswater that she realised that she was bereft of her knickers, tights and bra. The workmen must have taken them. Beryl smiled to herself. 'Souvenirs, I suppose.' She snuggled deeper into the back seat of the cab.

5

'Don't worry, Reuben, they're not lethal.'

Shirley Merchant had peeled off her stockings and was dangling her suspender-belt in the air. She imagined Reuben might never have seen one before, except perhaps in a catalogue or a shop-window. She tossed it too carelessly over the back of the chair and added, 'Unless, of course I decided to change it into a catapault. I could adjust the buckles for length or distance then, couldn't I?'

'You could, I suppose you could, but there wouldn't be much power in the force. It wouldn't be of much use. I doubt if it would injure a sparrow.'

He dealt with her innuendoes innocently and left her totally disarmed. This increased her attraction to him. She had watched him undress. He had done it rapidly and had jumped into bed still wearing his vest, underpants, and socks. He had left the light on and she lingered, getting ready for bed like

an experienced tart. Reuben remained unmoved. Shirley
assumed that he couldn't see much anyway as he had removed
his glasses; he was fiercely myopic. She stripped naked,
switched off the main central light but illuminated her own
bedside with a small paraffin lamp.

'Are you asleep?' she asked.

'No, of course not.'

'My husband was short-sighted. He wore glasses.'

'Is he dead?'

'No, gone off.'

'Gone off?' Reuben sat up and faced himself roughly in
her direction; he could make out the pool of yellow light
round her, but little else.

'With a cellist; a lady cellist in the orchestra. He played the
violin, so now they scratch together.' Shirley chortled somewhat bitterly.

'I'm sorry,' said Reuben.

'Yes, so am I. They are both Party members so the rift has
the blessing of the State. I've accepted it now, though. Flat-
tery from women always got my husband horizontal. I was
the first to flatter him. I was never unfaithful to him. Do you
believe that, Reuben?'

'Yes, Shirley, I do. Are you going to read a little?'

'If you don't mind, I think I shall. The light won't affect
you will it?' she asked. Her tone had lost its abrasive edges.

'No, I sleep easily, quickly. I'm a light sleeper, but I drop
off quickly. Good night.'

Shirley tried to meander through a selection of Sufi poems
which she had borrowed from Isobel. Their finality offered
no balm for Shirley. Spiritual philosophy did not help her.
She shut the book, turned down the wick of the lamp and
blew out the light. Reuben, true to his word, was already
asleep. She heard the front door bang. More people had
arrived. Isobel and Harry would deal with the new arrivals.
She could think of nothing but what was involved within the
room where she lay. But was there any involvement there?

She could imagine one. Shirley found this prospect unattractive; better to try to make one. If she failed, then what was lost? She had enough humility to recover. Rejection of all kinds were not new to her.

An hour later she climbed into Reuben's bed. She waited for him to push her out or request sweetly that she return to her own. He did neither. What he did do was to turn and face the wall and make more space for her on the outside of the bed. She snuggled into his back; his vest tickled her nipples. His clothing provided the only sensation that she was aware of. She slipped her right arm over his waist and he casually encased it under his arm. She coiled one leg of his hairy calf and touched a woollen sock with her foot. She waited. Reuben was soon asleep once more. Shirley felt comfortable. 'Perhaps that is what I need,' she thought. 'Just a bit of comfort — a bit of proximity.'

Her snoring also left Reuben unaffected. He was a quiet, accepting man.

Margaret and Isobel had listened to Beryl's information. Beryl was astonished by the calm manner in which they received it. Harry had settled Beryl down for the night. She had no objection to sharing a room with Madge, who had whooped with glee at the prospect.

'It's just like *Girl's Own Paper*, I don't suppose you've ever heard of Angela Brazil and people like that?'

Beryl hadn't but Madge's enthusiasm was infectious and they had parted for bed as though they were going for a midnight bun party in a lower sixth form dormitory. Isobel said good night to Harry and Margaret and made her way to her room. It was miniscule and might almost have suited an anchorite. It had once been a large linen room. Harry had removed the wooden slatted shelves and there was now room for one narrow single bed, one chair and a recess that held her clothing suspended on a wire line. This was where Isobel Quirk lived. The walls were white. There was one paraffin

lamp and the one concession to decoration was a picture
post-card of a Mogul prayer rug. Nature in all patterns of red,
green and ochre abounded on the card; Isobel often looked at
it. No human form of decoration graced the room. Isobel
prayed through Christ and she was sure that He would not
object to the prayer rug. She talked with Him a long time, in
fact, she slept before she was a quarter of the way through
her agenda. It had been a tiring day and the week ahead had
boundless challenges in store for her. She slept heavily.

'Oh, it's all so rich, Margaret, it's all so rich. I wish Stella were
alive to be in it all.'

Harry Wintner burnt his lip on his cocoa and said 'Ouch' as
he addressed Margaret Davis. Forewarned, she blew on hers
before drinking a little. The light-brown froth from the cocoa
had lined Harry Wintner's top lip to give his grey, ashen face
a temporary pale, brown moustache. He let it linger a while
before licking it away.

'Would you like a biscuit, Miss Margaret? A digestive? I
fink this is all very rich, very rich. Everyfink looks as though
it is working out tops at present.'

Harry's long training in serving the aristocracy had left
him with an admixture of terms which did the splits between
the East End of London and the set of people who were
ready for a minor county fox-hunt. His pleasure was manifested only when his pale eyes ignited.

Margaret took another sip of cocoa and ignored the digestive biscuit. She was half-concentrating on her finger-nails.
She was usually busy with her hands but it never seemed to
detract from the singularity of her power for listening or her
concentration for participating in conversation. She applied
some apple-green nail-varnish to the thumb on her left hand.

'So far, all, or most, of the teachers are here. I have not
approached Pauline Bontil as yet; Leslie Murt will come of
his own volition, without overtures from me. Marjorie Prentice
has proved her alienation beyond doubt. Beryl would not,

could not, lie. It's very sad about Marjorie.' Margaret shook her head and stroked her forefinger with the tiny nail-brush.

'It smells like pear drops.'

'What?'

'The varnish, Miss. We used to eat lots of pear drops when we were children. They were boiled sweets shaped like pears. Is Mrs Prentice that bad?'

'No, I think she suffers from silliness and jealousy. They must be fearful handicaps to have to live with.' Margaret blew on her nails.

'They are both constant so she is never without them. Eventually, I'm sure that the two qualities will kill her. At least you know where you are with a genetic disability. Is this smell putting you off your cocoa?'

Harry had left his cocoa standing and a skin had crept over the fast cooling contents. He took a quick, long gulp to put Margaret's mind at rest. The intricacies of their caring for one another knew no bounds. They did not have to make sacrifices, it came naturally to them both. Mutual adoption in their case was beyond form-filling, blood, or religion. His paternity like her filial obligation was based on admiration, need, and love. Margaret felt most fortunate that she had been able to choose her father, surrogate or not.

'So far, then, there are six of us.' Harry drained his cocoa.

'Yes, by next Thursday, there will be eight adults and twelve children. Are we prepared, Harry?' Margaret finished her little finger.

'I have worked out some plans of employment for the week-end. We must begin early. Isobel wants us all awake by seven and if we all carry out the duties allocated, we should be prepared. We hadn't expected Beryl so soon, so we shall have an extra pair of hands.'

'Beryl is very adaptable — a surprising woman in many ways,' said Margaret.

'I like all of them, a rare bunch of people,' said Harry Wintner.

'There are more rare people than you might think, Harry. I'm going to bed now,' Margaret announced.

'Leave the alarm calls to me.' Harry spoke quietly.

She kissed the top of his dull grey hair and left him to clear away the mugs.

At one time, all the children had arrived for school by special yellow buses. They had been picked up at an allocated point near their homes at an allotted time. The parents had seen the children on the bus in the morning and met them off it in the evening. More or less this meant that most of the children arrived at school punctually between 9.15 a.m. and 9.30 a.m. This was an arrangement which opened the commencement of an exciting, integrated day, and took a great deal of strain and stress away from parents whose livelihoods were dependent on being in a position to work. They were able to organise their own lives accordingly as well as care for their afflicted children. It was still by no means easy, some managed to cope better than others, but most of them had not succumbed to despair and after a period of anxiety managed to live in their own worlds of acceptance. Their wounded children had not, to any large extent, set them apart. Sacrifices of a very personal nature, like most forms of real courage, were left un-heralded. However, they did not go unnoticed by Isobel Quirk and her colleagues who praised them daily.

After the Government of National Unity was formed things became more difficult. Stringent economies had been made in accordance with the Campaign for National Strength. At first the buses were reduced in number. This meant a 'double run'. Some children arrived at 9.30 a.m., others came in later at 10.30 a.m. The school-day was battered by economics. Eventually, the buses were lacerated altogether and the parents were responsible for delivering their children to school as well as collecting them. Isobel had objected. Mr Ostanley had said it was a step in the right direction as it was dangerous to 'mollycoddle' anybody. This simple economy caused great and lasting anguish. It received little publicity from the strictly monitored national radio, television and newspaper media which deemed time and space should not be given to unproductive minority groups. Isobel's staff put in more time, and sought to alleviate the suffering engendered by this action.

Margaret Davis had suggested at a staff meeting that the only way to deal with it all was to be joyful. Isobel had been perplexed, but Margaret's plan had worked well. A celebration was held every morning. Every morning was tantamount to a jubilee.

The singing and chanting, some said it sounded like cater-wauling, could be heard from the uppermost floors of the flats that leered over the school. Initially, the inmates of Delphinium, Laburnum, and Chrysanthemum towers had thought that the school was holding some strange kind of evangelical revival meeting. The clapping and singing was of a euphoric nature and the throbbing of drums had also been heard. It was a strange cacophany, but most pleasant to the ear and, much to Mr Ostanley's regret, there had been no complaints. He had broached the matter with Isobel with subtle veils of criticism, but she had all but snapped at him.

'You're not suggesting that the guardians would wish to quibble with God, are you Mr Ostanley?'

He had let the matter rest there, the government wanted no more quarrels with the Church. The Catholics and the Quakers were already being very sticky indeed over some issues. There was no point in upsetting the whole lot of them.

Mondays at school were especially vivid and Margaret Davis took to the hall floor bedecked for the occasion. Her fashion sense was individual in that what was 'in' at any particular period did not affect her. 'Clothes should not reflect a sense of time,' she had declared to Madge Wragg. Both women had every reason to bolster each other in this way as one was approaching forty and the other, by State reckoning, was almost ready for the grave. Margaret chose to wear what she liked and on this, the first Monday of what was to be an eventful week, she was graced and garlanded with an outfit that might have sought to meet the needs of a multi-racial wedding. Our bride gave no sops to the symbolic purity of white — from top to toe she appeared rampant in colour; fluorescent.

Encircling her hair was a bridesmaid's coronet of former years made up of daisies, lily of the valley and faded bluebells. Her cobra-like arms clattered as she whirled them about her. Rings sparkled on her fingers and bangles and bracelets flew up and down her wrists. She had added (with the aid of felt-tip pens) a bird to the tattoo on her left arm so that now a peacock showered its tail feathers up to the top of her shoulder. Around her neck she wore a collar of tiny bells which had come from Morocco. The bells jingled faintly as she moved. A royal-blue peasant blouse with flowered embroidery about the edge of the low neckline enshrined her torso. Below the waist she wore a patchwork flared skirt that had as many colours as Joseph's coat. The skirt reached her calf-muscles. The legs were bare but silver sandals encased her tiny feet and three or more bracelets entwined themselves round each small, well-formed ankle.

Margaret stood in the centre of the hall. The sight of her startled no one. She had begun to clap her hands as the first trickle of children and parents came into the hall and sat themselves down round its sides. Madge Wragg followed the rhythm on a tambourine, while Reuben Goldman played twiddly bits on a recorder. Shirley Merchant strummed amateurishly, but with effect, on a guitar. The rest of the staff clapped. Pauline Bontil's eyes were drawn to Margaret's hair. It often changed colour. It was now a bright orange and had the appearance of a huge mass of grated carrots. It looked appetising rather than appealing. And this was how Pauline viewed Margaret — appetisingly. Both teachers had arrived early that morning and their conversation had left Pauline, dowdy Pauline, hungry for more of it.

'In a way, I think I admire the Magdalene more than any other character in the Testaments.'

Pauline was both startled and intrigued by Margaret's statement. The weather had been dealt with before they had removed their cardigans and no more preliminary small-talk observations or pleasantries were exchanged.

'Perhaps it is that she offers comfort to my past way of life. Of course, you understand, I have never done anything like that for money. Never. Yet, I have been accused of being a tart, I was only fourteen at the time.'

'How dreadful, Margaret, how unfair. Whoever accused you of that?'

'Oh, a headmistress; the headmistress of the school I attended,' said Margaret as she applied some mascara to the other eyelash. She blinked and the eyelash took on more profound proportions.

'Heavens,' gasped Pauline. 'What had you done?'

'Dyed my hair — I still do. It's bad for the roots, but the children like it.'

'So do I,' added Pauline vehemently. She was not aware that she was not telling the truth.

'Today is very special, so I really went to town on it last

46

night. Brilliant, isn't it?' Margaret fluffed the frizz with her green finger-nails.

'Yes, it is brilliant,' Pauline agreed truthfully.

'This is my St Mary Magdalene Day, I'm wearing musk oil scent too.'

Pauline was well aware of the heavy odour which had initially caused her nose to twitch, but like most things about Margaret she had become accustomed to it.

'I hadn't realised that you were interested in the saints,' said Pauline, fingering her St Christopher medallion.

'Oh, I am. He's been struck off the register,' Margaret pointed at Pauline's medallion.

'Dear me, I didn't know,' said Pauline.

'Never mind, there are plenty of others. Do you know about St Zeta?'

'Who?'

'St Zeta; she might have worn a frying-pan round her neck as an emblem. I'm not joking. St Zeta was a kitchen drudge, just think, a kitchen drudge who surely joined the highest orders in heaven. She's amidst the martyrs.'

'Martyrs!' Pauline placed her St Christopher in her handbag; her eyes glowed and her body tingled with excitement.

'Yes, and just think, most of us here have the opportunity to seize martyrdom.' Margaret applied some orange lipstick and pressed her lips on a tissue. 'That is, if we choose to seize it. You might say it's on offer.'

'I haven't heard anything about the offer.' Pauline pouted and spoke in a petulant tone and then began to sulk.

Margaret reassured her. 'Well, Pauline love, we weren't sure if we should tell you. I feel confident about you, but the others ...'

'How anyone could think that I would want to deny the constant love of Jesus ...'

At this point other teachers had begun to arrive. Pauline felt thwarted in that their conversation had been forced to end prematurely. However, Margaret had whispered to her before she trailed the musk oil into the hall.

'I'll include you at break-time.'

With the odour of sanctity pervading her nostrils and with these words still ringing in her ears, Pauline continued to stare at Miss Margaret Davis who opened the week with hypnotic fervour. Isobel was welcoming the last of the parents at the door and Margaret launched forth into a climactic point in the assembly.

'I've got one of God's children in my arms,
I've got one of God's children in my arms,
I've got one of God's children in my arms,
One of God's children – in my arms.'

The parents joined in with the singing, and the orchestra of Shirley on guitar, Madge on tambourine, Reuben on recorder and Leslie Murt on drums gave a rousing backing. The handicaps of the children were as varied as nature itself: there were children with some speech, and children without. The genetic handicaps were there: the microcephalics' heads bobbed and chortled as they sang and the hydrocephalics smiled and nodded slowly. Quadraplegic children, whose intense spasticity caused them to flop like rag dolls if they were not held, were jigged on knees. The mentally and physically maimed made their noise, their actions and created their own happiness. Margaret orchestrated it.

'Let's have that verse once more.' She twirled about as the music continued and picked up a smiling, four-year-old quadraplegic from the knee of a parent and danced with him into the centre of the room, then did a side-step across the room and thrust the child into Pauline's arms. The verse was repeated and Pauline, flushed with honour, joined the centre of the floor with Margaret and chirped her contribution.

Isobel descended the eight steps into the hall as the song ended. This was the signal which indicated that all the children had been welcomed in and that it was time for parents to leave.

48

'Grand chain — all link up,' Margaret shrieked.

Somehow everyone managed to attach himself to the next person.

'All together — now the last time, lift the roof, mean what you sing. Mean it. Believe it.

We've got the whole wide world in our hands,
We've got the whole wide world in our hands,
We've got the whole wide world in our hands,
We've got the whole world in our hands.'

The singing stopped and everyone clapped and applauded. Isobel joined her colleague and friend in the centre of the hall. Her manner of communication was very different; she spoke with a quiet gravity and intensity which commanded attention by the integrity of its delivery.

'Today is the first of June. Happy month everybody.'

'Happy month, Mrs Quirk,' the chorus ricocheted her greeting.

'Monday, the beginning of a new day. Happy day everyone.' Back came the chorus, 'Happy day, Mrs Quirk.'

The different teachers began to collect their classes; the children swarmed about them like chicks about hens. However, such was the intensity of the routine and ritual, such was the excitement of welcoming the new day, that the chicks were guided to their rooms without undue mishap or mayhem. Only when Isobel noticed a group of children left behind in the hall did she realise that Marjorie Prentice was absent. It was not like her to be unpunctual, so Isobel correctly assumed that she had absented herself for the day. There was no point in relaying her concern to the waiting parents.

'I'm taking Class Green today; Mrs Prentice may be in later. Please don't worry, leave them with me.'

If they were with Mrs Quirk there was no cause for delay. The last of the parents dispersed quickly; most of them had to go to work — a handicapped child brought extra expense which often entailed the need for both parents to be working.

Isobel waved them good-bye. She escorted the class to its room. A frown scudded across her brow. Where could Marjorie be? Staff always telephoned in if they were unable to attend. The phone had not rung, and Marjorie was not present. The needs of the children erased her anxiety.

She had been standing immobile for perhaps two hours or more. Occasionally, she would sit on the toilet seat or perch on the edge of the bath. No attempt had been made towards ablutions; her hair was unbrushed and her hands and face unwashed. She was still in her dressing-gown. From time to time she would stare at her own image in the mirror, only to move away or recoil from it as if in disbelief or horror. A blue-bottle fly began to buzz about the room and this began to hold a total fascination for her. She watched it whirr about and eventually return to its original point of departure which was the frosted-glass window. It would beat its legs, wings and antennae against the window before taking off for fresh flight. Marjorie watched the fly repeat the operation time and time again. The creature caused an abstracted smile to crease her face. She continued to watch it and made no attempt to dress.

Quite suddenly she moved quickly. She seized the toilet-roll and pulled off a couple of metres. She squeezed the paper into a ball that her hand was only just large enough to hold. It was like clutching the head of a mop. The fly buzzed about her head; she sat quite still. It settled on her forearm then flew away. More audacious than before, it settled on her brow and explored the features of her face before returning to the frosted-glass pane. Marjorie rose quietly and approached the creature. She held the paper mop a centimetre away from it. She paused to consider the creature once more. Then, slowly, deliberately, she moved the mop onto the fly and trapped it. The buzzing stopped. Marjorie tittered and pressed harder, harder. She heard the squirting and squelching sound as she spattered and crushed the creature on the pane. She withdrew her instrument of execution and considered her achievement. Traces of blood, wing and thin spider-like legs were indelibly printed before her eyes. She half-screamed and broke the sound by pushing the soiled toilet-paper into her half-open mouth. The acrid taste of the remains of the fly made her recoil from her action and hurl the paper away from her. Her dressing-gown belt had fallen to the ground.

All her movements from now on were enacted as though she were a mechanised robot taking orders from elsewhere. The superstitious might have suggested that she was possessed. She stroked the pink yoke of her night-dress over and over again, fingering the expensive embroidery, smiling as her fingers undulated over the material. She stroked the flimsy coverage on either arm. First one, and then the other, she picked up the dressing-gown belt and let it hang round her neck and fall over her breasts. Once more she stared at the fractured remains of the fly on the window-pane. The laughter grew; she turned and lifted up her night-dress and made an obscene gesture to the mirror. More laughter, higher, more shrill; she made her way to the landing and stood at the top of the stairs giggling and shrieking. Somewhere the laughter ended and the sobbing began. It racked and shook her whole frame. In the last stages of exhaustion, she tied one end of the dressing-gown belt round her neck. The other end she tied to the banister rail. She leaned over; there were less tears now. The worst was over — just fall, just fall.

It took Marjorie Prentice almost half an hour to die. The belt slithered along the banister and did not come to a halt until it reached the knob on the landing. Marjorie felt the jerk at her neck but remained quite conscious. The tips of her toes just reached the ground-floor. She could not reach the knot above her head, nor the floor beneath her feet. She struggled to do both. Pulling both ways, manipulating both ends, she managed to strangle the life out of herself. Before her face turned purple she bit through her tongue, thus severing her own torment forever.

Isobel received a telephone call in the late afternoon to say that Marjorie had died from natural causes.

'Did you say from natural sources, or natural causes?'

'Causes, Madam, causes.'

'I see, thank you for letting me know.'

Isobel remained still. She would tell no one the news until the evening. No point in upsetting the atmosphere at the school — the day had to progress. Half an hour later, Leslie rang the bell three times and the children trooped into the hall for the collective good night and dismissal. There were always apologies from parents who were late in picking up their children.

'Don't worry, it's not your fault.'

Isobel repeated the phrase over and over again.

7

'I'm joining you. I'm coming tonight. Oh, Mrs Quirk the excitement of it all just leaves me, well — I have no words to express how I feel.'

Pauline had burst into Isobel's office seemingly breathless with anticipation. Isobel looked up from the forms in front of her, she was awaiting a telephone call from Mr Ostanley. She had contacted him shortly after hearing the news of Marjorie's death. Pauline teetered like a schoolgirl entering her first infatuation. Isobel did not have the time to listen. She interrupted her with sweet curtness.

'I'm pleased, Pauline. Shirley and Margaret will help you with your effects. I shall see you later. Now, I must say good night to you.'

Pauline was not hurt. 'She sounds just like a Mother Superior', she thought.

In total obedience, happier than at any time in her life,

Pauline nodded her head and went dutifully to join her order.

Leslie Murt had entered the room and sat himself down just as the telephone rang. Isobel could hardly wave him out, and clearly he was intent on staying. He was an intuitive man.

'Hello, yes, Mr Ostanley, I asked for the sad news to be relayed to you. Yes, quite naturally we are all very upset about the matter and most shocked.'

Shocked and upset about what? Leslie lit his pipe and remained where he was. Isobel had used the collective 'we' so presumably she meant him too.

'A heart attack? I've never known Marjorie to have had a day's illness in her life. I would like to see her.'

'No, I don't think that I am being indelicate.'

Leslie noticed that Isobel's pallor had gone quite white; he knew that anger affected her in this way.

'If you are suggesting that I put undue strain on her and caused the attack which resulted in her death, then say so.'

'I'm sorry, I must have misunderstood you, then. No, Marjorie never complained of chest pains. Quite the opposite in fact, she always purported to be healthier than anyone else here.'

'Well, if I cannot see her, then her next of kin should be contacted.'

'I'm sorry, Mr Ostanley, there *is* a next of kin, an aunt who lives in —'

'Senile? She's not sixty-five —'

'No, I'm not being obstructive, but a colleague's death —'

Leslie choked on his pipe. How long had Isobel contained this information? Poor girl, she was suffering. If only she would let him hold her. If only ...

'I cannot see how or why her burial should be within the bounds and confines of State secrecy. I do not believe that the true circumstances of Mrs Prentice's death have been established —'

Isobel looked up and stared blankly into Leslie's face. She

54

held the receiver away from her face. He could hear its faint burring tone.

'He has put the phone down on me. He has just cut me off,' she said.

'You have been doing the same to me for weeks.' Leslie's answer jarred her already jangled emotions.

She folded her arms on the desk in front of her, placed her head on them and wept with relief. He did not move, for his own sake he dared not touch Isobel. He knew that he never would. He ached to stroke her short-cropped hair so gently with his hand. He looked at his hands, large, beefy. 'Useless,' he thought. He continued to look at his hands as he spoke.

'I know what is going on anyway. The last of your cohorts was recruited today at break-time.'

She dried her eyes with a paper tissue. 'How did you know? Eavesdropping, Leslie?'

'Couldn't avoid not knowing. I was sitting in the lavatory. It came through on the intercom. Pauline is very close to ecstasy. I hope you realise that you are risking your lives.'

'Other lives are at risk, Leslie, so why should ours matter so much. We have planned it all as carefully as is possible.'

'I know that, but must you act so very much alone. It's a bit arrogant of you. You should be attempting to enlist the support of other groups.'

'Other groups? I have found out that I am only effective by being parochial. This stance, this plan, call it what you will, is best kept within the "family". In any case we would all find it difficult to affiliate. We are all in one house for the same cause, but our reasons for being there are different. I suppose you could term all of us marginals.'

'Marginals?'

'We don't fit in anywhere, not quite, we all have our rituals but none of us are bound by usual traditional ties.'

Leslie grunted.

'Is that why you kept me out of it — because I am bound by traditional ties?'

'You are married, Leslie. There is your wife to think of.'

He reacted angrily to Isobel's patronage. She deserved it, and accepted it in the constructive spirit in which it was offered.

'If I had thought of my wife, I would not be here. When I was appointed here I came for my own needs, not hers. I'm fed by her and we sleep in the same bed. Our communication has not gone beyond that for the past fourteen years. Our children are married — all gone, and that's good. She is supplied with all the money she requires, her hair is done twice weekly and she attends two clubs for ladies each week. I do not interfere with her bridge parties. She no longer questions my thoughts, our attempts to converse are pathetic, limited to the need to mow the lawn and change the washer on the tap. Therefore we speak to each other about twice a month. If I am not marginal, then what am I? You have not categorised the others yet you choose to categorise me.'

'I'm sorry,' said Isobel.

'So am I, but I'm not sorry that I love you.' He blurted the words out.

'I am,' said Isobel.

'Explain then,' he said.

She paused and closed the folder in front of her.

'Go on, it's time you did. Tell me something that I don't already know.' He sat back in the chair and folded his arms defiantly. He had never challenged Isobel in this manner before. Within school he carried out his duties with spaniel-like devotion and protection. She had never heard him growl before. She did not wish to hurt him, but he had given her little choice. He had deliberately chosen to cross the road without looking and had insisted on facing the consequences.

'Leslie, for very personal reasons I made a deliberate vow to remain chaste many years ago. I have kept it and I enjoy keeping it. If I ever chose to break that vow it would not be broken with you. However, it is unlikely — as I say, I am happier this way — I prefer not to be touched.' She stood up thinking that her cruelty would put an end to the conversation. Leslie waved his large hand and signalled her to sit. To her surprise his expression reflected no injury. On the contrary, he looked somewhat relieved. He was actually smiling.

'I'm not asking to touch you. I've done enough touching in my time. I ask to be about you, no more than that. You have given me no new information. I have never been tortured by hopes or fantasies. My position is not that much different than yours except that you have to make your love alive, whereas mine is living. I see it every day, it's quite enough. You cannot deny me that. I am joining you. I know the location of the house so there is very little that you could do to stop me.'

'I won't stop you, Leslie.' Isobel spoke with relief and smiled.

They smiled and beamed at one another before breaking into gentle laughter. Leslie stopped it.

'I think that we should talk over practicalities.'

'Name some,' she said.

'When do you plan to disappear?'

'Next Thursday; we leave after school. We take the twelve special-care children with us.'

'Can you trust all the parents?'

'We have to. They have all been informed and are sworn to secrecy. They do not know our whereabouts, but they are entrusting the children to our care. They have little choice. It's us or it's the guardians. Even if they are questioned they will know nothing. They will have no answers to give. They can pass on blame.'

'Transport?'

'With your car added we have no more problems. We can manage.'

'You are bound to be discovered, isolation is never successful.'

'It can stop a disease from spreading, we are ready for any virus attacks.'

57

'I know that you have an arsenal, it could come to that too. You're not afraid?'

'Of course I am, but I have been afraid before.'

Her truthfulness often surprised him.

'I still think that you should enlist, make other contacts.'

'We are prepared for a state of siege.'

'You cannot survive a siege without the expectancy of eventual relief.'

Isobel leaned back in her chair, her way of saying that she wished to listen. Leslie was talking good sense. He was talking beyond the present and the immediate future. Her stance before was based on defiance — she did not know what this might achieve. Leslie was talking of hope. This was important.

'Messages must be got out — they have their propaganda, we must issue ours,' he said.

'Our telephone has been removed. It would have been bugged anyway.'

'No,' he barely gave her time to finish. 'We must use more natural forms of communication.'

Isobel was puzzled.

'Do you have wood available? Is there a shed in the garden?'

'There's an old gazebo that would easily convert into a shed, but we don't really need one. There's masses of storage space within the house. It's very large and spacious. The attics have been converted into three beautiful dormitories for the children. Don't worry about storage space for supplies, we are prepared; we have water too.'

He had begun to shake his head.

'I want a pigeon pen.'

'A pigeon pen?'

'Yes, a pigeon pen, some pigeons, some balloons, and at a pinch, I wonder if Shirley and Beryl could produce some kites.'

Isoben snapped her fingers.

'I've got it.' She jumped up from her seat. 'Message carriers — all of them.'

'Yes, it's far-fetched, but it's a try.' He was pleased with himself. 'Could be that dying this way might be fun.

'It's not our choice how we die,' she said quietly.

'I'll join you on Wednesday.' He rose to leave, but turned as he reached the door. 'What about the rest of the school?'

'It's due for closure next Friday. We are all to be replaced. Ostanley has already informed me of the matter. You heard the other news, about Marjorie?'

'Yes, I'm not surprised. Are you?'

'I don't know. I never will know. I feel angry.'

'Use the anger, store it.'

Leslie waved and closed the door behind him.

'I'm very lucky,' thought Isobel. She pondered on her good fortune only to have her thoughts interrupted by the insistent ringing of the telephone at her side. She looked at it coldly. She had never liked the instrument. In a few days' time she would never have to listen to it again. She let it ring and waited for what seemed hours for it to stop. It clanged remorselessly on.

'Hello, it's me, Margaret. You have to get to Letitia Passmore's without delay. I'll meet you there. Shirley Merchant may be going there too. She mustn't be left alone with Letitia. She doesn't understand. Can you hear me?'

'Yes, I can. I'll make my way over straight away. I'll see you there. Good bye.'

In her haste to leave the office to see her cancer-ridden ex-colleague and friend, Isobel left the telephone off the hook. There would be no more calls coming in for a time. She climbed into her car and clutched her cardigan about her. The evening had begun to chill. She shivered and released the hand-brake. The engine broke into life. If only ending life were as simple as beginning it. Poor Letitia. But why was Margaret so afraid of Shirley arriving before they did? There must be some good reason. She pressed her foot harder on the accelerator and in spite of the chill opened a side window of the car. Isobel felt the need to breathe.

They had taken away all that could be taken from Letitia
Passmore. They had taken away her small flat. Removed her
privacy. They had taken her away from children and her colleagues, forced her to retire from her job. Within months of
leaving her post, the cancer began to eat away at her and her
flat and pension were absorbed by her placement in a home
for the ill — it was called the Inevitable Eventuality on the
form. People in Letitia's position were no longer allowed to
leave death in the hands of fate. They were removed to homes
where they were expected to die as quickly as possible. If
they could not accept this a working team of dedicated doctors
took the responsibility for them. However, the medical team
considered that a woman of Letitia's sagacity and intellect
should be quite capable of doing or applying the final graces
for herself. She had duly been informed that she was expected
to die within the week. No food had been offered her, but

liquids were readily available whenever she chose to ask for them. On the small dresser next to her bed was a glass of orange juice and three yellow capsules in a plastic container.

'Well, Miss Passmore, it comes to us all some time, and when it does, better to face up to it than cry or lose any sense of dignity. I know that you wouldn't want to feel a burden on yourself and your friends and there does come a time when all of us must consider what we have left to live for.'

The matron rearranged the carnations in the vase. Letitia could smell them, see them.

'I enjoy the flowers,' she said lamely.

'Yes, dear, but even they don't last forever. They bloom and make way for the next crop. The water in the vase won't help their cause. By the end of the week, they'll be well past it. Just think how nicely poetic — you and the carnations fading sweetly together. When you're ready, swallow your pills and sniff the flowers. The last experience you'll have will be their sweet odour. That would be nice. I'm leaving the capsules here for you — it's better if you do it of your own volition. Leave us smiling, Miss Passmore, it will be nice to remember you that way.'

Letitia could not recollect hating anyone apart from the matron. It is true there were people she had disliked, but this woman she detested. She hated the woman so much that she had not taken the capsule just to spite her. The idea of taking her own life did not revolt her. Indeed, she had been, and still was, a lifetime atheist. But there were things that she still enjoyed despite her helplessness and agony. Flowers, for instance. Her friends who saw her regularly still gave her a reason to be alive. Isobel, Shirley and Margaret, her doves she called them, all three filled her dying frame with well-being. Letitia had one day left before the decision of taking her life would be decided by the medical guardians. Letitia opened the plastic container and held one of the capsules in the palm of her hand. She found the colour quite attractive. The idea of popping it into her mouth as though it were some sweet filled her with rancour and indignation. Letitia was very tired, she felt very ill. Regrets were no longer of consequence. Letitia Passmore had never experienced despair. Still she lingered over the capsule. Even in her present state she remained without that particular quality which would facilitate her putting the capsule to her lips.

If she left matters another day then the issue would be settled by an injection. She had always been deeply sympathetic to children who feared immunisation in school. Some of their cries now rang through her head. In spite of the cajoling, the promise of a piece of chocolate as a reward, the cuddling and the cossetting, some had continued to whimper and cry. 'Not the needle, Passmore, not the needle. I don't like the needle.' Now she had a choice of facing the needle herself. And what was her reward afterwards? Certainly not a piece of chocolate — and Letitia believed that what bits of heaven were available to her she would know about in her present life. No, she did not want the needle, the idea of an injection in her present circumstance appalled her. She took the other two capsules from the container.

The Final Rest Nursing Home was staffed by four doctors, twelve nurses, a matron, and three black ancillary helpers. There were from eighty to a hundred patients in the home. The fluctuation in numbers could vary as much as this, particularly if they had a good spate of deaths. Sometimes life became easier if the dying could see to the operation themselves. It had been as low as sixty-five in one week. However, this had been a difficult and exhaustive week.

Matron had observed to the chief nursing orderly, Mr Ramp, 'We have a right old bunch this week. Some of these old girls would hang on to the edge of a cliff for a month unless you stamped on their fingers. I think a week is much too long to give them to decide. Look at that old Mrs Creasey, she was in a frightful mess. We were having to change the sheets and turn her over at least four or five times a day. But would she take the capsules?' Matron shook her head. 'No, she would not. Senile old cow. We couldn't have coped with her for a week in the state that she was in. I slipped the capsules in with her orange juice. Not strictly ethical, but I'm sure people turn a blind eye nowadays.' Matron laughed. 'Do you know, her last words were a complaint. She said she had never liked marmalade. She said her orange drink tasted bitter — like marmalade. Some people never appreciate what you do for them. That's a fact. Still, I don't suppose one could have expected much else from an old pea-brain like Mrs Creasey. Not an ounce of intellect in her; she hadn't the sense to realise what a useless nuisance she was. The Passmore woman surprises me — a retired head teacher you would credit with more sensitivity, wouldn't you? She's gone the whole week. Almost every day I've expected the capsules to be gone. I've worked on her and the psychiatrist has had a word with her, but she hasn't touched them. Well, tomorrow we'll be rid of her; capsules or no, her time is up. She's got a false smile. I don't think there is any point going near her any more. I've done my best and no one can do any more than that, can they?'

Letitia contemplated the three capsules which lay in the palm of her hand. She let them roll round a little, then she clutched them tight. Better not let them roll on the floor. She opened her palm once more. Perhaps that would be her answer — if she held them long enough on her outstretched hand she would grow tired and then they would fall to the ground. She would have no decision to make. She continued to stare at the yellow capsules.

Margaret arrived in the room four yards ahead of Shirley. The two women had raced one another up the steps along the corridor and into Letitia's room. Letitia did not complain.

'Let her take them,' said Shirley.

Margaret shook her head. Shirley stepped towards her.

'Well, give them to me then.'

'What for?' Margaret asked.

'You know what for. I'll give them to her.'

Letitia smiled at the two women as though they were deciding arrangements for a picnic. Margaret closed the door of the room and stood with her back to it, thus sealing the entrance of the door with her body.

'You are not having them, Shirley. You are not going to give Letitia anything,' said Margaret. She clenched the capsules tightly in her fist.

'Don't be bloody stupid, she'll have the white-coats around her tomorrow morning if you don't give me them.'

Shirley moved towards her.

'Keep away,' Margaret rasped.

'Why?' Shirley could not understand why Margaret had taken up a posture which resembled a bitch protecting her puppies.

'Keep away. Letitia is not an animal. I won't have her put down. I won't have her destroyed.'

'Who the fucking hell do you think you are? She's not going to be left to agonise for another minute.'

Shirley grabbed Margaret's wrist. Letitia propped herself up in bed – it was a gigantic effort that almost exhausted her completely. However, she was much delighted and enthralled by the show which was passing before her eyes and was intent on not missing it. It was very exciting.

'You'll take away every bit of meaning to her life if you give her these.'

Margaret got the words out as Shirley struggled with her to take the pills from her clenched fist. She twisted Margaret's arm behind her back. Shirley was a strong woman.

'Stuff your empty rhetoric, hand them over. Letitia needs sleep.'

She jerked Margaret's arm much further up her back. In her younger days Margaret Davis had trained as a tap-dancer and an acrobat. Sometimes on application forms she wrote that she was a lapsed soubrette. This puzzled many people, but as the word sounded French, it impressed some with its mystery. Shirley was more surprised than Margaret when she found herself flung sideways as Margaret's small foot hooked around her ankle and brought her with a thud to the ground. Shirley possessed no acrobatic skills, nor was she adept in any form of martial art, however, her tenacity could not be denied. She clung on to Margaret's arm so that Margaret's agility did not save her from ending up in the same position as Shirley. Both women were now struggling and rolling about the floor.

Margaret attempted to sling Shirley off her and throw the pills out of the window. Limpet-like, Shirley clung on to any part of Margaret's twisting and kicking body that was available. It was a difficult task. Twice Margaret hurled Shirley from her with some force, and on one of these occasions Shirley thumped her forehead on the polished wooden floor, leaving her semi-concussed. Margaret leapt to her feet and lunged for the window. Somehow Shirley had grabbed her ankle and brought her down. Shirley hung on to the ankle and Margaret kicked out at her with her other foot.

'Let me go, you fool,' gasped Margaret.

This was the mayhem that Isobel witnessed as she entered the room. She closed the door quickly behind her. One glance at Letitia settled her priorities. The sick old lady was shaking her head from side to side, her eyes appeared to be focusing somewhere in the back of her head and a horrifying rattling noise seemed to be coming from her throat. Isobel took Letitia's hand, it was warm and Isobel felt a slight pressure of recognition.

'Letitia, Letitia, it's me, Isobel. Letitia.'

The two women on the floor stopped their struggle and crawled on all fours to the bedside. Both knelt on the opposite side of the bed from Isobel. Isobel repeated the phrase.

'Letitia, it's me,' Margaret echoed her.

'Letitia, we are here, we are with you.'

'Passmore, sweetheart, it's us,' said Shirley, fingering a fast swelling bump on her brow. They waited like this.

Letitia's eyes still roved about her skull and the rattling noise shook her body. Then, for a moment, for a fragment of time, her will, her life, returned to her. The eyes focused on the women before her. A lull in the rattling occurred. Letitia smiled. Her lips moved, the effort of moving them was similar to hauling a ten-ton truck or lorry. The words came out, not whispered but quite clear, quite distinct.

'What a marvellous, marvellous way to die. To see your friends fighting for your life. It's been so invigorating, so exciting, I'm so happ —'

The eyes lost their focus again, the rattle became heavier. It ceased. Letitia's head flopped to her shoulder as though it belonged to a rag-doll. The eyes stared at nothing, sightless, yet still blue. Isobel felt the pressure leave her hand and she let Letitia's fingers slip from her. Margaret closed the old lady's eyelids and Shirley took a hairbrush and titivated the long thin wisps of hair so that it fell in tresses about her shoulders.

'Is she dead?' Shirley whispered.

'Quite dead, she's gone,' said Isobel.

Margaret had begun to cry in a noiseless fashion. She left her position and stood near the window. Shirley joined her and placed an arm about her shoulder and held her head to her breast.

'Your hair is tickling my throat.'

The frizz had an almost electric effect on the skin. Margaret pulled her head away, but Shirley's arm stayed about her.

'You'd better let me put some cold water on your brow, it looks fierce,' said Margaret, tears still welling from her eyes.

She took a paper handkerchief and dabbed the bruise with cold water from the tap in the sink positioned to the left of the window. Isobel straightened the bedclothes and watched her two friends. One looked as though she had been through an all-in wrestling match, while the other one's face resembled that of a jaded clown. The tears had played havoc with Margaret's eye-shadow and mascara and the brine had left streaks of blue and black rivulets about her face. She looked permanently startled. Isobel joined them.

'You'd better let me have them,' Isobel spoke quietly.

'What?'

'The capsules.'

Margaret handed them over and all three women stared at them. Isobel turned on both taps at the sink. They watched the capsules swirl and disappear. Shirley began to make a harsh, low wailing sound, Margaret's tears began to well up once more. The two women clasped and held one another. Isobel looked out from the window. An elderly lady was being carried on a stretcher towards the entrance. Isobel sighed and placed her 'arms about Shirley and Margaret who were still entwined in grief. The three of them stood like this for two or three minutes. Isobel spoke first.

'We had better leave,' she said, calm but firm.

The other two obeyed. They left without glancing back at Letitia. True to form Letitia had managed to satisfy everyone, even in the manner of her dying. What was most important was that she had also satisfied herself.

The note was carefully placed between a pot containing some flowering geraniums and a small milk-jug. Some of the petals from the plant had fallen into the milk. Leslie fished them out before he read the note. 'Dear' had long since been abandoned, the notes were purely for information purposes.

'I have left some chicken in the fridge. I've cut some slices off the breast, you will see them on the plate. Don't touch the main carcass as I want to use it for a Chicken Marengo tomorrow.'

'What the hell is Chicken Marengo?' Leslie paused to light his pipe.

'There are two plastic cartons, one has coleslaw, the other potato salad. Use some of both if you want them both. There's some nice fresh bread and you know where the cheese is. I've left the butter on top of the draining board so that it will spread more easily. Don't forget to put it back in the fridge after you have used it. It really is such a price now-adays. I would boycott buying it if it weren't for you.'

'What a sacrifice.'

'After or before your meal could you collect some meat from the butcher on the corner. You can call in at the back, they are expecting you. The deep-freeze is getting low and buying bulk saves a lot. I told Mrs Grainger at number 27 that you would have a look at her lawn-mower. The wheels go round but it skims the grass without cutting it. I said that you would know what was wrong. Their eldest son has just been appointed as bank manager in Southampton. He's done very well. Mrs Grainger says he is 31, but I seem to remember him being older than Jean so he must be all of 35. Still, he has done well.'

All her notes were like this, a section on what had been done for him, a section on what he ought or must do, a section that took the form of her thoughts mashed up with a mixture of the two previous sections. It would be a relief if ever she wrote a note that surprised him. Freda held no surprises up her sleeve, or up her knickers.

'I ought to be back about 10.00 p.m. I'm at a whist drive in the Parochial Hall. It's in aid of preserving elephants, I believe; the old people tend to slow things up a bit, so I may be a bit late. I'm surprised – some of the prizes are very good. I hope I don't get stuck with any doddery partners. That's what baulked me from winning the last time – remember? I had a letter from Jean today. She and Michael are going to Spain for their holidays. The Costa Brava. You might mention it to Mrs Grainger when you are looking at her mower. After all she is our daughter.'

We never see her, she's a stranger. Leslie puffed at his pipe.

'I have left a clean shirt out for you tomorrow, it's the one with the blue pin-stripes on it. Could you call in and collect the tomato plants on your way back from school? I have to go to the hairdressers in the morning and in the afternoon I'm attending my "See your London" course. We are viewing the postal services tomorrow. To finish up we are having tea at the top of the Post Office Tower.'

Leslie Murt chuckled to himself, in spite of his phlegmatic ambience, he possessed a vivid imagination. The thought of Freda and fifteen others like her being slowly spun round as they drank their tea amused him. What if the machinery went wrong and it really began to whizz about. My God, that would make the permed hair uncurl.

'Don't forget to feed the cat and leave her a saucer of water, not milk.

Freda'

He had met her at an afternoon tea dance. Freda always maintained that they had been introduced to one another at a party. She came to believe this. He had introduced himself to her on the floor of the Palais de Danse during an 'excuse me please' quick-step. When the tempo changed to a waltz he thought that he might be able to get a bit closer to the pale blue shiny satin dress, rub against it, and if he was lucky, peep down the enclave of her sweetheart neckline and glimpse the beginnings of her breasts. But Freda kept at a distance, so that he had to be satisfied with the feel of her bottom under the shiny material and gaze at her even features. The hollow of her throat was protected by a small heart-shaped pendant.

'It opens up.' He had bought her a glass of lemonade during the short interval. She pressed the side of the locket. It flicked open. On one side was a small photograph of herself.

'Who's the other space saved up for?' he had asked.

'I haven't met him yet.'

Leslie misinterpreted this and took it that Freda had a romantic outlook. This appealed to him greatly. It was only later that he realised that their courtship, their nuptials, their children, their mortgage and what proximity they had ever possessed, she plotted and set out like a recipe from a pernickety cookbook. Only so much of this and a fragment of that will eventually give you this. Throw in all the right ingredients, measure carefully, mix and you have a happy marriage. Freda believed she was happily married whereas Leslie had not felt married for years.

Leslie loved women. Their physical aspects, no matter what the proportions and placement, still gave him thrills of excitement. Large breasts, sagging couplets, small pointed ones, they all appealed. Bums, low slung ones in jeans and pear-shaped ones draped in cotton, all gave him momentary joyous contemplation. He liked the smell of women too. At one time his outlook was entirely chauvinistic: you were well mannered with women and if you were lucky they would let you have them. You would be allowed to touch and enter the crock of gold between their legs. He had never been handsome, but by a combination of protectiveness, reasonableness and postured conformity, he had managed to have five or six women before he had met Freda. Once when feeling desperate, he had paid for it.

'Five pounds straight,' she had said.

Leslie paid up and went through the performance. Afterwards she had thanked him.

'It makes a change having it straight.'

He had not understood her because she had taken the money first. None of his other women had thanked him for taking their drawers off. Quite the contrary, on three occasions he had apologised profusely for getting carried away and one of the girls had worsened the situation by saying that she hadn't realised he was like 'that' and never wanted to see him again. The others had found boy-friends. His rather miserable record was why without much enthusiasm he found himself at the tea dance of a Saturday afternoon. He did earnestly and truly feel an urgent need to know a woman — apart from the other thing.

It was intensely difficult to come to know Freda as she was very busy in the ensuing weeks getting to know all about him. She demanded an inventory of his personal details. What was his job? Where did he live? What did his parents do? Who were his friends? When she had taken him home her father, who was a retired policeman, had wanted to discuss Leslie's prospects. After some time Freda and her parents decided that Leslie's prospects were good and Freda placed Leslie's photograph in her locket. This flattered him, it was the nearest he ever came to her breasts before they were married. If any physical advances were made he was strictly and firmly cautioned.

'Save it, Leslie, save it until we are married.'

He had never asked her to marry him. Things just built up that way and although Freda was no raving beauty, 'saving it' sent him into the wildest fantasies of passion for her. He never doubted that she had something to save for him. In this sense he began to consider her special, and himself fortunate. Once, between her clenched teeth, she had pulled away from him.

'You know where that leads to, Leslie. I thought we had been through all that.'

Eventually, after six months the clenched teeth led him to the altar. A smart honeymoon was spent in Cornwall.

'Lovely setting,' Freda's mother had enthused.

The rocks and the wild sea did not arouse any deep-seated or latent passions that might have stirred within Freda's frame, and the bracing sea air blessed her with a heavy head cold after three days. She had let him jump about her for the first two nights, but never moved from her horizontal position. Afterwards when it was over, she had murmured, 'There now, does that feel better?' It was as though she had treated him for some ailment. With the onset of the head cold, he was asked to refrain on the grounds that she didn't want him to catch it too — he would have willingly shared her sneezes but acquiesced. He had always been a reasonable man.

This had been his undoing, because he had bowled reasonably on ever since. His career had progressed accordingly, not that this mattered particularly. They had moved house three times, each time the house became slightly bigger than the

one before. Freda had always said that she wanted to get
back to office work but somehow had not left the starting-
block. Their first daughter arrived after two years and Freda
dutifully held that she must devote her full attention to all
her offsprings' rearing. It was an excellent execution and she
managed to produce copper-plate versions of herself. Leslie
had never liked his own children over-much; he found them
less interesting and much less beguiling and honest than the
injured children he had chosen to teach. Freda was not aware
of this; she and her children mistook Leslie's apathy and distance for urbanity and self-satisfaction. They misjudged him
severely.

His sexual relationship with Freda had ground slowly to a
halt. He had not complained when she requested separate
beds while she was suffering the 'change'. The 'change' did
nothing for her, but during this period Leslie himself entered
a strange round of promiscuity with women of forty-five
years or more. He was astonished at their passionate physical
response and for the first time concluded that Freda was a
cheat. Nothing more than a respectable cheat. He had once
made love to a teacher in a telephone kiosk. Decorum forced
them to remove the bulb first. He had burned his fingers on
it. What followed was awkward but thrilling and the peri-
patetic teacher did not complain about her laddered stockings. Strangely, Leslie was never fulfilled, he never wanted to
know any of these mature, loving ladies. He hated feeling
predatory, so he stopped his ramblings. It was at this point
in his life he met Isobel. They had competed for the position
she now held. It was her coolness which had captivated him
at first — her coolness and her legs shrouded in criss-cross
black net stockings.

He had expected to be rejected when he applied for a post
as her deputy. For him professionally it was a move sideways,
he was going from one deputy-headship to another. Freda
had called him a silly crab. He even had to travel further to
work and there was no rise in status or salary. This had been

brought up at his interview; perhaps it was why Isobel had supported his appointment. He would never know, she never talked of such things. She ran the school compassionately, efficiently, she ran it well. He admired her enormously but she maintained her aloofness. One day, after he had been there for over two years, she came to him in his class-room. The day had been punitive, disrupted by staff absences, distraught parents, and the *grand mal* fits. She looked tired, drained, and the lines about her eyes were stamped on her like cobwebs. He had absorbed two classes all day, he had covered play and lunch duties and had no break. It was almost the end of the day, he was telling and singing a story. She had come in the room and touched both his hands with her own.

'I value you Leslie. I value you,' she had said.

The intensity of the delivery of the words had knocked him sideways. He ceased to yearn for her but from that moment he began to know her. Fulfilment with a woman had come late to Leslie and now that it had arrived the nature of its existence devastated all his previous fantasies. It was enough for him to be near Isobel Quirk. He neither asked for nor needed anything more, he was both content and happy in his adoration.

Should he leave a note for Freda? He had packed his suit-case. Bugger the lawn-mower, the meat could stay at the butchers. He was not hungry. He slung his raincoat over his arm. Could he leave after twenty-five years of marriage without so much as a word of good-bye? He thought of the good-byes at the assembly at school — only an hour ago they had occurred. He had watched the corners of Isobel's mouth twitch, this was all that she allowed to indicate that it was almost certainly her last. Some of the other teachers had been less restrained. Pauline Bontil, Margaret Davis and Beryl Cranford had all wept. Reuben Goldman and Madge Wragg could not bring themselves to wave away the coaches as they left. Shirley Merchant had clenched her fist as she waved.

Isobel twitched at the mouth but waved as she always had done.

The special-care children had been kept back and if the bus-drivers missed their presence they asked no questions, expressed no comment. Posters had already been stuck on the outside walls of the school informing parents of a 'temporary closure' due to architectural faults in the building. Isobel and the staff knew this to be a lie — they had always had architectural faults. It had been fun living with them. Some of the parents had looked intently into the faces of the staff during that last morning get-together. That was all they did; it would have been unproductive to do or say anything — but a look, that was something different. The expression on the faces of the few children that Leslie transported to Bayswater varied from discomfort to glee. One of them needed his incontinent pad changing and the other enjoyed his anguish. He handed them all over quickly to Shirley and Reuben who were allocated to be responsible for dormitory placement. The day ought to have been tense. Somehow, the tension never came. Ostanley and his cohorts had not come near the school and the whole operation had been neat, swift and cool. Just as Isobel would have wanted it to be.

Leslie placed his raincoat over the back of the chair and used the same pencil his wife had left behind after writing her letter to him. The sheet of paper was clean on the other side. He wrote.

'Dear Freda,
I have gone, I have left for good.
Leslie'

There seemed no point in saying any more. She had access to his bank balance, his pension rights, they owned the home — or rather she did now. She was welcome to it. He had £50 in his pocket and carried a few belongings in a hold-all bag. He shut the door behind him. He would leave the car behind. It might prove to be an encumbrance in a state of siege. The prospect of the days ahead thrilled and excited him. He waved the bus to a halt, he apologised to the bus-conductor who grumbled and growled when proffered a £1 note.

'Keep the change,' Leslie reassured him and patted the man's hand as he took the ticket from him.

'I'm not supposed to, yer know.'

'Disobey. Go on, disobey.' Leslie could plead.

He had to change buses so that when he arrived in Bayswater he possessed £48, a few clothes, and 15,000 balloons.

10

'I would prefer not to be in a position where I might have to kill. I mean it would be better if I were not armed. I wish only to protect. I'm sorry.'

Pauline fidgeted on her chair in the large sitting-room where all the company were assembled.

'Don't start the meeting with a worry, Pauline. We should open our meetings as we always do.'

Margaret turned towards Isobel, who sat in a high-backed chair near the French windows. It was mid-June and slight drizzle had begun to fall on the garden. The grey light behind her obscured her features; all that most of the company could see of her was a silhouette.

'Isobel, are you going to open the meeting?' Margaret asked.

Isobel's voice came from the shadowed wing-backed recesses of the chair.

'I don't know if I am in any position to do such a thing. If we need a chairman, then it might be better to elect one. It would be more democratic.'

'Chairperson,' Shirley interjected.

'Don't be so —' Madge Wragg began to speak, but stopped. Not on account of her teeth, but because she had learned that economy was the most important commodity of most meetings that she had had the misfortune to attend. Freewheeling discussions bored her and at such times her wig made her scalp itch.

It was Leslie Murt who broke what might have become an uncomfortable silence. Isobel had not moved, she sat and waited. As far as was possible at this moment she was in control of her own destiny. This did not give her *carte blanche* to plot or plan other peoples'. She might even experience relief if someone else were elected to take her position. Perhaps they might even conjure up a rota.

'We are still a school. We wouldn't be here if we weren't. Your position is not open to election.'

Isobel had never heard him speak so adamantly. He was worried. Did he fear that they might elect him?

'Ahem, what is my position in all this?' Harry Wintner was a little confused.

'New school-keeper, very responsible and difficult job,' said Margaret.

'We should vote, we should vote on something,' said Shirley.

'We vote on whether we are or we are not a school. It is as simple as that. It is not at all complicated.' Reuben licked his lips. 'Isn't it important to recognise what we are, what we are as a group?'

'All schools have to be officially recognised,' said Beryl.

'We are the officials,' said Margaret.

The assembled voted unanimously to remain a school. Isobel left her seat and leaned against the large marble mantlepiece which surrounded the fireplace. For some reason she still did not feel satisfied — that was it, unsatisfied, not insecure.

'That still does not mean that my appointment as head teacher is axiomatic.'

'We are still the same school, the interviews were held years ago.' Leslie looked to her and frowned.

'Of course we are the same school, all we have done is change the building. Since when did a building constitute a school. If we were in igloos or tents we would still be the same school. Stop this ferreting Isobel. Do you want us all to raise our hands for you to let you know how good we all think you are? You're the head teacher, now get on with it.' Madge Wragg snapped her teeth shut. She was clearly annoyed with the proceedings.

'All agreed?' Reuben called out.

'Agreed.' The chorus was louder than warranted.

Isobel quietly returned to her place near the French windows. She was pleased that they could not see her expression. Even she, at this moment, was having some difficulty in hiding her own feelings.

'It seems to me that the first thing we should review is the allocation of our responsibilities. These are usually based largely on need, and our prime need is the children that are now in our care. At this moment, probably for the first time in their lives, they are being left unattended.'

Isobel had opened with a structure. Leslie loved to listen to her, she had slashed the excitement from their situation and given it profundity.

'Most of them are asleep.' Shirley was a bit irked and was making some kind of lame excuse for the group.

Pauline stopped her fidgeting and rose from her seat. 'I'll go up.'

'Thank you, Pauline, but it might be better if you stay for a few more minutes.' Isobel spoke, Pauline sat.

'Someone, no, more than one, two of us must be with the children night and day. They will need feeding, changing, exercise; if we are not careful it will be so easy to get caught up in events and forget what led us to these events. The children led us all here. I propose that two or three of us should be allocated to cater for all their needs. It will mean that the persons involved will probably have to sleep in the dormitories. It will be demanding and fatiguing, I think we can all recognise that.'

'Proposal put,' Leslie bawled.

The hands were raised in unison.

'Can I go now?' Pauline was anxious to get to the children. 'The other strategies will not concern me too much, I just want to care for the children. I very much need to care. I cannot do this in any other way. I realise that some of you are capable of expressing your concern differently. I'm frightened, but I will be fine if I'm left with the children.' She had stood once more and nervously straightened the creases in her skirt.

'Go now, then,' said Isobel.

'Thank you,' said Pauline.

'Good girl,' Leslie Murt called after her as she scuttled quickly from the room.

'I'm the other one aren't I?' Beryl asked a question, then answered it. 'Yes, I am. You all know my views about the cycles of life. Not all of you agree with me, but I have always felt that you respected my views.'

Shirley winced as Beryl spoke. Once during a school lunch one of the cooks had inadvertantly served a pilchard on Beryl's salad. She had sat at the dining-table next to Shirley and stared at the remains of what was a fish. She was quite distressed, but had overcome her revulsion and kindly offered the fish to Shirley.

'Oh, eat up, Beryl, it's been in a can for years. It won't feel anything now.' Shirley's response had been feckless.

'I cannot eat dead flesh. The thought of a carcass, tinned or otherwise, makes me feel sick.'

Beryl had left her meal and Shirley had not been able to tackle the pilchards that day. Normally, she was quite fond of them.

'I can defend life, but I am not able to take it away from

anything in any circumstances. It is me, I am the one to share duties with Pauline.'

'Yes, I think you are,' said Isobel who admired plump, awkward Beryl. Margaret nodded in Beryl's direction and smiled.

'Ahem, it would seem that some individual arrangement must be made with regard to you then, Miss?' Harry Wintner directed his eyes just above Beryl's head as he spoke.

'Individual arrangements?'

'As to what you eat, Miss.'

'How clever of the man,' thought Isobel.

'I'm the cook, I take it that you are a vegetarian. If so, then I will be happy to comply with your wishes.'

'Oh, how very kind of you,' Beryl picked up her handbag from the floor.

'What a nice, thoughtful man your father is, Margaret. Thank you, Mr Davis, sorry, Mr Wintner. I'll see how Pauline is getting on. John Middleton usually needs to be turned on his side once he has dropped off to sleep.'

'Here you are, dear. There's one for you and one for Pauline. The lime is the best flavour.' Madge Wragg handed Beryl two boiled sweets as she left the room.

Isobel waited for Madge who had begun to offer sweets all round. Three were accepted. The crackling of the cellophane wrappers eventually came to a halt, only the occasional sucking sound could be heard above the patter of the rain. Madge began to cough and splutter a little.

'It's gone down the wrong way.'

Margaret thumped her back and Isobel commented.

'Welfare, communication and defence; these are the main topics for tonight's discussion. Shall we deal with them in that order?'

'Defence should come first,' said Shirley.

'I don't think so,' said Reuben.

'You can't have any form of defence without welfare or communication, hold on to your horses, Shirley. Reuben is right.'

Margaret and Harry nodded their heads in agreement with Leslie, and Madge assented by waving her hand and pointing to the chair.

'Not only do we have to consider the children's welfare — but our own. As time progresses it may be necessary to formulate rules, but for the time being, if we progress as a school, these should not be necessary. However, in the allocation of duties it should be borne in mind that all of us should be keeping a gleaning eye on one another. We are all about to be subjected to new and unusual forms of stress. It is essential that we look after one another accordingly.'

'Love one another,' Margaret almost sang out the words.

'If you wish to put it that way, yes. I think that it will either demand more of us or oddly, considerably less of us, than it did in the previous building. You have expressed it better than me, Margaret. Perhaps I was afraid to use the word. You are right, it will be imperative for us to love one another. How we do that is to a great extent defined by what each of us will become or already has become.'

'All this is going over my head. Can we get down to the nitty-gritty?' Madge was not going to change much whatever happened and she knew how irritable she could be if she became tired. Harry Wintner patted her arm. She immediately felt better and clicked a smile at him.

'Our food supplies here could last us up to four months or even five. Harry is responsible for all meals and must be given full co-operation. He has discussed this with me and I can give you a full assurance that he is most well informed on dietary needs. I must declare open agreement on one point.'

'Oh, oh,' exclaimed Madge. Things were beginning to ginger up a bit. She stifled a yawn and stopped scratching her head.

'There are eight adults and twelve children —'

Shirley interrupted. 'I thought there were fourteen children.'

'Two were absent.'

82

Iṣobel continued thinking 'They are absent gone, absent lost, absent dead ...'

'Eight adults and twelve children, this makes twenty in all. It seems far too much for one person to take on such a huge catering task. I realise that few of us here will have had much experience in this area, but Harry will need help.'

'I'm experienced. I spent some years as an assistant cook in a munitions factory from 1940 to ... oh, I forget when. I'd be more than happy to join Harry if he'll have me.'

Madge returned Harry's pat as she spoke. Isobel was astonished as Madge had often declared in the staff room that she never used the electric stove at home because she never had cause to cook anything. She always ate a hearty meal at school. Harry reacted mildly, almost apologetically.

'I'm sorry this part of the operation has to take two of us. It looks as though your bellies are going to rest in the hands of two senior citizens.'

'I wouldn't say that, my hands haven't touched anyone there for years.' Madge did not like being called an old-age pensioner, whatever semantics were used. Laughter all round took them on to the next business.

'Leslie, I think you could tell us about the next section. You know far more about it than I do. It's time for me to listen and learn.'

Leslie got up from his chair and stood at her side. Although one arm was draped casually over her lap he noticed that her other hand gripped the chair's side. The knuckles shone white. Did she ever relax?

'My main feeling about all this business is that we should avoid the danger of writing ourselves off.'

'Write ourselves off. We're putting ourselves on, not off.' Shirley rushed the words out and Isobel wondered what the cause of her over-reaction might be. She appeared to be under more strain than anybody else.

'Wait, my dear,' Reuben spoke soothingly.

'What do we look like to people outside of here? Or how

do we look? What picture will they have of us? How will they view us, or be seen to be viewing us? A bunch of cranks? A group of anarchists? A set of pathetic eccentrics? A group of ageing revolutionaries?' Leslie paused. 'All of us here know. We all know that we are none of those things.'

Margaret faltered, unsure of her ground she waved her arm limply. A bangle clattered.

Leslie had achieved his aim; they were all less self-satisfied.

'I don't think we should be so selfish. There may be others who feel as we do. Others who think differently from the State. I think that we should try to let as many people as possible know why we are here. If we don't then the State guardians will give their version of us. You don't have to rack your brains to know what that will sound like. It's most important that we should attempt to give some account of ourselves to people outside. With luck, we may even enlist support.'

'Who do you think might support us?' Reuben placed his head in between his hands and balanced his elbows on his knees.

Leslie's brow furrowed; he tugged at his ear-lobe and then filled his pipe. He'd won his audience. Let them wait a bit.

'If I knew the answer to that it is conceivable that none of us would be here. Yet, there must be sympathisers around, it's just that they have gone to earth like foxes do when they're being chased. If they sniff us out, they could leave their dens. We will need help. Isolation remains splendid for only a short time. In the long term, it offers no hope.'

'How are we to let people know? There is no way that we can get out.'

Margaret was interested. She respected Leslie Murt — in spite of the fact that he had once pinched her bottom when they were cataloguing equipment in the stockroom at school. She had been shocked. He had apologised immediately saying that it would never happen again. It hadn't happened, but Margaret saw to it that she did no more bending near Leslie so as to avoid further occurrence. She did not want to present him with an opportunity to lapse. She had discussed the matter with no one. It could have been anyone's bum, her's just happened to be there at the right time in the wrong place. It was the position and the timing that had invited the pinch, not the person.

'I'd thought of a number of ways of making contact. Perhaps other people might like to put forward other suggestions before I sound off.'

'No, let's hear yours first,' Shirley was calmed and spoke more gently.

'I have brought a radio transmitter along with me — but it won't be too long before they block any messages that I send. In any event, our messages ought to be individual and peculiar to us as well as representing us as a group. There are ways in which we can all get our messages across.'

'How? We can't fly out and sail back in again. The gate is barbed and the walls surrounding us are 8 foot high or more. How much is that in metres? I can never get used to metrics. Are you serious? I've been called an old bat before now, but I can't see how me or anyone else here could scale the walls after tonight. We're enclosed — we can't fly out can we?' Madge asked.

'No we can't, Madge, but others can.'

'What others?'

'Pigeons,' said Leslie.

'They are out of the question. They need a lot of training and nurture, there would not be sufficient time to do much with them. It would take at least a month and they would absorb more time than we have to spare. Pigeons have to be tended. I once had a lover who was a pigeon fancier. Lovely birds, all blue, grey and pink. When they fly over your head there is a strange whirring noise. I don't know whether it comes from their wings or their throats, or both.'

Margaret shook her head sadly. 'No, they need too much tending, too much love. We won't have it to spare.'

'In that case we must settle for inanimate methods. Balloons and kites are the answer.'

'Good God, Leslie, we are not having a jumble sale, or a fête here, it's not a bloody party or a celebration,' said Shirley.

'In some ways it is,' murmured Margaret somewhat dreamily. She was still regretting the fact that the pigeons would be useless.

'I have 15,000 balloons and enough gas to float them. Messages can be attached to all of them. One general message could be carried and one individual one. Of course, they will settle and land at random. It's just a chance we have to take as to where they will land. If we release them in batches of 500 they are bound to attract attention.'

'Some might fall on arable land,' said Isobel who was picturing the sight of the balloons.

'Pardon?' Madge had lost track of the conversation.

'Some of them, even if it's only a few hundred, may fall into the hands of sympathisers. And then there are always the curious, they waver.'

'They will certainly attract a lot of attention. I think that it is a very good idea,' said Reuben.

'We could float posters, I could work out how many balloons would be needed and gauge the suspension.'

Shirley had been infected by Reuben's enthusiasm. Isobel had noticed that when Reuben proffered opinions, Shirley almost always tempered her abrasive remarks. He affected her like valium, or a mild tranquilliser that took away pain of the biting edge without removing the bite. This was good as Shirley's bites were often productive. Leslie muttered through his teeth which were clamped over his pipe.

'Excellent, Shirley, excellent.'

She had led him on to his next strategy.

'Posters ought to be on the outside walls of this place. They should be on them now. They ought to be plastered with them. If what Harry and Reuben have told me is true, then warning posters ought to be posted up tonight. It's imperative.'

'Whatever for? We were forced to come here. Damn that lot outside, why should we worry about getting them up tonight? What's the rush?' asked Madge.

'The lawns between us and the walls are detonated with explosive. They are a mine-trap for any would-be trespasser. To walk across the lawns would mean instant death to anyone who tried it.' Reuben spoke with a flat tone, his voice void of excitement or vicarious pleasure. It was as though he were discussing notations and harmony for recorder and piano.

'I think we should warn before injury or death is caused, we might harm an innocent otherwise. Our purpose for being here is not to injure or harm. The explosives are placed to protect. The posters outside should be up tonight.' Isobel glanced over her shoulder. The sky had darkened, it would soon be twilight.

'That is a job for Harry and me, it comes under the category of defence,' Reuben interrupted Isobel's short reverie with the dwindling daylight.

'Don't forget me, I am in the defence section,' Shirley appealed to him.

Isobel intervened.

'Our categories of responsibility are bound to blur, Shirley. It's obvious that you are going to be involved in communications too. Your artistic attributes and your practical knack of making or mending everything under the sun is going to prove invaluable to us. Margaret can help you with the posters. From what Reuben has said we will need them completed before the night is over. I'm sorry to give you such short notice, but we will often have to make decisions like this. Not day by day, but hour by hour, it isn't going to be easy.'

'You have to change one quicker than you think. Posters would be torn from the wall in seconds. We will need to paint directly on the walls. I am the only one who could achieve this swiftly and effectively,' said Shirley, not with arrogance but with a firm conviction that what she was saying was unassailable.

'It will be very dangerous, Miss — er — Mrs — er — Shirley, only Reuben and me can plot our way across the lawns. We have a pattern, it's like a Chinese puzzle. One route must be kept to all the time. If the track is veered from, it would mean death for anyone chancing their luck. We can't afford to risk your life, we have learned the route by heart. We do not feel that we should share this knowledge. I'm sorry,' said Harry.

'I'll keep one step behind Reuben. If I have to, I'll crawl on all fours. I'll track him, stalk him like a leopard.'

Shirley threw back her head and tossed the fringe of hair from her eyes. Margaret watched her; if Shirley had sniffed the air in feline fashion it would not have surprised her. Isobel was not prepared to challenge her demands.

'Do you agree to this, Reuben?'

Isobel had to wait for his response which was not immediate. He stared at Shirley. She did not take her eyes from the thick lenses and it was he who averted his gaze.

'Yes, Shirley can follow me,' he said as though he were committing both of them for much more than one nocturnal adventure in slogan painting.

'We must wait for darkness.' Harry looked out from the window.

It had stopped raining. Margaret joined him at the French windows and slipped her arm through his. The two of them looked out on the lawns.

'Where will the children play?' Margaret looked at the green grass and blenched at the thought of what it could cough up. In March and April it had sprouted croci and daffodils. Now the same earth could belch destruction. She shuddered.

'The concrete yard behind the kitchen and the large space

at the back of the conservatory are clear. These are the areas to which the children will be confined if they are taken out. Four of the children are immobile — we have brought the matting with us.' Isobel's capacity for noting and covering details that might be missed had not waned.

Shirley got up from her seat and stood next to Isobel, her arm draped over the back of the chair. 'I had better get the paint and brushes ready.'

From her new vantage point, Shirley could see that Isobel was fatigued. Margaret left the window and sat back on her haunches on the other side of the chair.

'Give me instructions as to lettering and size and I'll begin on the posters. OK Shirley?' she smiled into the face of her friend.

Leslie scrutinised the trio. If he were an artist, he would have loved to record them, a photograph could not have interpreted the tapestry that the three of them now represented. (Isobel always refused to have her photograph taken — an odd quirk of hers.) He looked at the group through the smoke haze that encircled his head. At the centre of it all sat the love of his life, taut, repressed, endearing. Was it possible for a man like himself to feel maternal? That is how he felt. Reuben broke the lull in the interchange.

'It is after nine-thirty now. We will need to be organised by midnight. It will be safer to commence the operation in the early hours of the morning.'

'Excuse me, I'm sorry to interrupt, but it's Hyacinth Lemkow, she has begun to fit. I think it's a *grand mal*, her breathing isn't too bad, but the convulsions are heavy.' Beryl Cranford delivered her information with her head popped round the half-open door of the sitting-room, purposefully restraining her agitation and anxiety. She closed the door behind her, and her head disappeared as though she had been a cuckoo clock. Isobel sat still.

'I'll close the meeting now. Tomorrow Reuben and Harry will discuss defence. What each of us will do if we are attacked.

I'm sure that you are all tired and some of you still have a long evening ahead. Now if you will excuse me, I must attend to the matter in the dormitory. Good night.'

She left them in this formal way. They were not surprised.

'The first balloons will be released at 11 a.m. tomorrow,' said Leslie.

Margaret signalled to Shirley and the two prepared to leave the room.

'You will need cover,' Reuben called after her.

'You sound like a cowboy, Reuben. Are you offering cover?' Shirley called over her shoulder.

'Yes, yes.'

Shirley stopped and faced him from the doorway. 'If you are offering cover Reuben, then I will feel safe.' She smiled once again, happy to leave and prepare her paint pots.

Harry Wintner made cups of cocoa for the remaining assembled. It was his way of stating that the meeting was over and other things needed to be done. However, the group needed refreshments and accepted it readily. Leslie Murt mused aloud. He slurped over his drink noisily.

'It's funny, it's very funny how three women like those three could be so close to one another. They have nothing in common. It seems a miracle as to how they all got to know one another.'

Madge snorted in irritation, she disliked romanticism if she were not perpetuating it.

'Nonsense, children brought them together. They brought all of us together. What is so miraculous about that? Oh, Mr Wintner, I've moved into the spare bed in your room. Beryl and Pauline need to share as their room is next to the children's dormitory.'

Reuben licked his lips and had to adjust his spectacles, Leslie spluttered over his cocoa. Harry Wintner seemed completely unperturbed.

'That's fine by me, Mrs Wragg. I prefer to share a room. I

was going to suggest it myself as we will be working together. Are you an early riser?'

'When there is a man around me, I rise with him,' said Madge. She picked up her bag. 'I'll go up and finish tidying my effects. It's years since I felt so happy, so satisfied. Good night everyone.'

The evening was over.

11

Mornings begin differently for everyone and Shirley and Reuben commenced theirs before light had begun to emerge. Reuben had thought it better to curtail numbers. In the event of accident or loss of life, it was better to minimise. Two could manage almost as easily as three. However, this did increase the effort that the two early morning adventurers had to put into their task. Much to her amazement, Shirley's earlier references to stalking Reuben like some female leopard were proving to be only too apt. Her present mode of movement was anything but comfortable and she had only covered what seemed to be one quarter of the distance between the lawn and the high wall surrounding the house. She crawled on all fours behind him. She wanted him to pause a little in his crawling as her breath was short and her heart was thumping. Unfortunately, she was unable to speak as clenched between her teeth was a paintbrush. She was champing at the bit like any thoroughbred mare, determined, dogged, but none the less well past the state of being comfortable. She sweated profusely and kept her eyes fixed on Reuben's behind which moved relentlessly on just a yard or so in front of her.

Reuben was more heavily handicapped. Suspended from his mouth was the tin of white paint. The wire handle pressed on his lower teeth and had begun to send jarring pains through his jaw. One of his teeth had begun to move and he was forced to push the wire handle further back into his throat so that most of the weight rested on his molars. It was impossible for him to turn his head, his only guideline as to Shirley's safety was her heavy breathing and snorting which to his great relief continued just behind his tail. Here at the first marker he must track immediately to the right, then right again at the next, then left, and then a straight line to the gate. If he stopped Shirley might relax and flop sideways. Better to keep at it and hope that her tenacity would carry her further than her physical strength could possibly allow for. He was beginning to doubt his own, but while she sniffed and snorted behind him he could carry on. If she should stop then he would give in. They would have failed.

They had passed the last marker, it was now just 10 or 15 yards straight crawl to the gate. Their crawl lacked its initial impetus, they wobbled from side to side and Shirley had lost some ground and was beginning to fade. He sensed this and sent a gargled call or half-shriek from the back of his throat. He reached the gate and rested his back against it, breathing heavily, jaws aching as if the bone had been removed, he stretched out his legs for Shirley who collapsed into his crutch in a sweating, panting heap. They lay there like this for some time, immobilised by exhaustion but part drunk with success. Shirley made as if to speak.

'Shush, shush,' he panted.

Shirley nuzzled her head into him where it lay. To her astonishment she felt him harden. She unzipped him and Reuben Goldman experienced the first shared sexual experience of

93

his lifetime without having to stir. True, his inert body shuddered and his legs twitched as Shirley's head bobbed backwards and forwards. Then his whole being seemed to shake. Afterwards he was flooded with a relief that he had never known. Shirley sat up and brushed the hair from her eyes. She was still breathless, he lay there, the epitome of ultimate relaxation.

'Wait awhile,' he whispered.

She nodded and grinned. He gestured her to move closer to him; with a single arm movement he held her head to his chest and they lay like that until the panting and sweating had subsided.

The high wall surrounded the house and Reuben decided that his best vantage point was to perch astride while Shirley daubed the paint on beneath him. She worked swiftly, effectively, not pausing for breaks. Reuben lay across the wall and hugged it close like some tenacious jockey. He moved along as she moved. At one point she chose to look up at him, not for one moment doubting that he might not be there. His head scanned the empty roadway, it swivelled this way and that. His legs and knees gripped the wall, his right arm dangled above her. In his hand he gripped a Luger pistol. She heard footsteps.

'Reuben,' she whispered.

'Keep painting,' he muttered.

The steps died away. If they had been witnessed, they would know of it soon enough. Shirley worked faster than before, she did care whether she lived or died and after the early events of the evening, death or the risking of it held much less appeal than before. Shirley was afraid.

The screech of cars or the wail of a police siren never fractured the air, the rain had stopped and the only sound that could be heard was the swishing of the paintbrush. The job was completed in under two hours and at 3.30 a.m. they were back at the gate. Shirley sighed with relief, turned to Reuben and beamed with triumph.

94

'We've done it.' She began to stride across the lawn. She felt herself being brought down with great force. Had something hit her? She struck the ground heavily. Dazed, bewildered, she felt a heavyweight pressing on top of her. Her head was being pushed into the earth. She struggled and managed to exclaim. 'What the hell —'

'Keep quite still, you may have touched off a detonated section of the grass.'

'I forgot, I —' Reuben pushed her face into the ground and half-lay across her head.

'It's clear now,' he slowly heaved himself from her.

Shirley spat out a mouth full of dirt and grass. Her nose was bleeding and she felt foolish. Reuben then commenced crawling and she followed him as before.

In the safety of their room Reuben wasted no time in getting into bed. This time he was quite naked, he had even removed his socks. Shirley hauled back the sheets.

'You had better wash your face,' he said.

Meekly, she was about to obey him. He called her back.

'No, don't bother, leave it as it is. Leave it. Shirley, come to bed.'

Shirley Merchant needed to be subservient. They slept coiled about one another, dirty, sweat-ridden, satisfied.

Harry Wintner rose shortly after Shirley and Reuben had retired. He needed little sleep and five o'clock in the morning was not an alien time for him to be awake. Madge made gentle snoring noises as he brought in two cups of tea on a small tray. They had pushed the two single beds together to make more space. Madge had said that Harry should not worry about this as she had been a married woman.

'No sex, just friendship,' she had said.

'If it happens, Madge, then it happens,' he had said.

'What?' she had asked.

'Oh, both of what you said,' he had replied.

Harry Wintner was never hypocritical. Madge's spirit

attracted him and eventually he might find some of her physical attributes attractive. Things often happened backwards so why reject them before they had begun?

He rattled his teacup but Madge slept on. She had removed her make-up and wig before entering sleep. Sucking and blowing came from her small shrivelled mouth, void of dentures. The sounds gently bubbled from the tiny aperture; she continued to slumber.

'You're a good old stick,' Harry Wintner muttered.

He stroked the fluffy wisps of hair that curled this way and that about her head. She opened her eyes and saw him sitting there. The sight of him did not startle her. On the contrary, she needed no gentle arousing, she was immediately alert.

'I brought you a morning cuppa, Madge,' he said.

She reared up to a sitting position and a little self-consciously raised her head and touched the fragments of her hair. He passed her the teacup.

'I've put one teaspoonful of sugar in it. I shouldn't worry about it if I were you. It looks fine to me, nice and soft, just fluff it about a bit and it will look like swan's down.'

No one had ever dared discuss Madge's hair before, they had hardly ever been given an opportunity. Madge was relieved that Harry had now mentioned it. He continued.

'Of course, if you feel better with the wig, then stick to it.'

'The main problem is that it doesn't always stick to me. It's begun to slip off lately. I suppose my head is shrinking just like the rest of me. Summer is the worst, it itches more then. To tell the truth, I've gone off it but I'd feel a fool if I left it off now.' Madge sipped her tea.

'It's years since a man brought me a cup of tea in bed. Have you done it before?'

'Done what?'

'Shared a room with a woman and brought her a cup of tea in the morning?'

'Ah, yes, I like a woman about me. There's another cup in the pot. We'll have one together.'

He replenished both their cups.

'It is homely,' she touched her hair. 'You don't think my own bits look too bad then?'

'No, no, I don't. It looks more friendly than the other,' he glanced at the dark-brown wig which hung on the corner of the dressing-table mirror. Everything about Madge was alive; strangely the wig seemed to hang on to some of her vivacity even when it was unattached.

'It looks like a kitten perched up there, doesn't it?'

'Believe me, it feels like one at times, I think I'll leave it there.'

Madge had been liberated.

'Shall I fluff your hair for you? I don't mind. I'd rather like to, that is, if it is all right with you?'

Madge was more than pleased to accept Harry's offer. She clambered from her bed and sat facing the dressing-table mirror. Her powder, creams and paints were all ready.

'Do you think I should leave all this lot off as well?' she gestured at the array of cosmetics.

'Oh, no, I like a bit of colour and scent, put all that on.'

Madge smiled coyly through her toothless jaws. It was years since she had experienced such spontaneous affection from the opposite sex. It made her feel younger than ever — about sixteen years in fact. He stroked rather than touched her hair and the net result was not unpleasing to her eyes or his. He inhaled her perfume as she gave hefty squirts of Daylight Magic behind each ear-lobe. Her throat was also given a good going over.

'Ah, that smells grand,' he said.

'I'll just slip my housecoat on and we can begin work. We can't afford any more time up here. I never thought that I could look forward to entering a kitchen.'

She stood up and turned gracefully to seek his approval.

'Do I look all right?'

'Lovely, my dear. Just grand.'

She took his arm, and with the utmost courtesy he led her

down for their morning's labours. They made an odd but dignified couple. Age had forced them both to realise the silliness of certain conventions and both had reached a period in their lives when all time was precious. They were reinforced with childish enthusiasm and an adolescent sense of wonder. The present sparkled for them. If you seized old age by the teeth (or the gums) it could be most attractive and full of surprises. It just needed a bit more effort to create them. Harry and Madge were more than capable of creating a sense of wonder — they had endless quantities of it stored within their creaking bodies.

In the kitchen they didn't talk much, they were busy and both of them had long since realised that it wasn't so much what you said that counted, but what you did.

'Blessed be the Holy Child Jesus, now and forever more. Amen.'

Some of the children were awake and Pauline spoke the words to them. She also spoke it to the ones who were still asleep. They didn't understand, but He did, so Pauline duly visited each bed in turn with her message. Beryl watched her from the doorway. Her upbringing had been anti-papist, she could not stomach dogma unless she had concocted it for herself. However, over the years she had tended to become less intolerant about the manner in which other people chose to believe. Pauline, like herself, believed quietly. Beryl appreciated this; evangelical rhetoric bored her and on occasions disgusted her. Beryl did not think that people should be exhorted to believe, although she did feel that they were missing out if they did not.

'The nuns always woke us up by sprinkling holy water on our faces,' Pauline had said the evening before.

'I think that would be a bit drastic. It would shock them,' Beryl had said.

'I wasn't suggesting that I should wake the children in that way.' Pauline told a half-truth. She had added, 'Would you mind if I woke them with a prayer?'

'No, not at all. It will be just a noise to most of them.'

'Yes, I suppose so,' Pauline had sounded a bit downcast. Beryl atoned.

'The inflection will mean something, what you feel when you say it is bound to mean something ... and I will be listen-- ing.'

Three times during the night the two women had alternated visiting the dormitory to check that all was well.

'It's like being called to evening offices,' Pauline had said.

'Why did you never take orders?'

'I've always wanted to be married, but no one ever asked me. I always wanted to have a child, but was never very keen on the idea of the process involved. I've never quite under- stood how sex and birth are correlated.'

'They're both violent,' Beryl proffered an opinion.

'How do you know?'

'I experienced sex and witnessed birth.'

'Oh, Beryl.'

'It was a long time ago. God has more meaning for me than any man now.'

'I've never wanted a man. Not really, not in that way. I always wondered if I might meet a man who would not want too much of that. I suppose that it would have been an unfair contract if I had ever made it. The situation is unlikely now but I would like a child. I mean I would like to have a child. To give birth. It's quite wrong of me to yearn.'

'I don't think that you say or do much that is wrong, Pauline.'

Having received absolution, Pauline had slept well.

Dressing the children needed a lot of concentration. The quadraplegics flopped about so much. Pauline finished her six first and helped Beryl dress the last one. The sheets on the bed were soaked in urine. The pungent odour swarmed into their nostrils. It had no more effect on them than a sea breeze.

'There, Jane, we'll soon have you comfortable, don't you fret my darling child.'

Pauline held the little girl to her while Beryl tore the sheets quickly from the bed. Beryl replaced the sheets and the rubber underlay. They placed the child back in between the dry sheets. Powdered, comfortable, clean, they tickled her cheek, she smiled. She understood.

They laid out the clothing at the bottom of each bed, it was easier working to a system, the shoes, socks, all the daily cover was neatly placed ready for the next routine. Things had gone well so far. Feeding would take place after they were all clothed. Harry and Madge had said it would all be ready in half an hour.

'You can say the other one if you wish,' said Beryl.

'The prayer that you keep repeating. I've never caught all of it.'

'Hail Mary full of Grace
The Lord is with thee
Blessed art thou among women
Blessed is the fruit of thy womb, Jesus.'

'And the other bit.'

'Holy Mary mother of God
Pray for us sinners, now and at the hour of our death.
Amen.'

'Now who is going to finish dressing them and who is bringing the food up?'

Beryl re-fastened the button of her nylon overall which fitted tightly across her breasts.

'You go downstairs today and we'll alternate,' said Pauline.

'Do you think we will ever leave here? I mean do you think we will leave alive?'

'I don't know. But should your faith allow you such a consideration? Isn't it important to take each day as it comes?'

'I'm not afraid now,' said Pauline.

'I can see that,' said Beryl.

She bustled out to be greeted downstairs by Madge and

Harry. The food trays were all prepared. She could manage two at a time. Isobel joined them. Her responsibilities had already begun to blur. She had to be where she was needed. Reuben and Shirley were to be called last of all. The warnings had been successfully posted without injury. The details and intricacies of the day had begun well. Pauline and Beryl, Madge and Harry had both grouped better than she could have possibly envisaged. The caring had commenced, it was still early. The hazards must come, which direction first? How far? What limits should defence be taken to? Pauline looked up from the child she was spoon-feeding. Looking at her, Isobel was aware that there could be no limits. She picked up the next sani-pad and applied it about the spastic thighs that lay waiting.

12

Every time John Ostanley looked at his daughters he was flushed with the same kind of tingling sensation that a brass military band sent through him. When it struck up for a parade, he felt very special in that he had fathered his daughters; his pride in them was boundless. The eldest was fifteen years of age and her sister was just two years younger. They were plain, neat, obedient girls who were rarely out of a uniform. During the day they wore their school uniform of grey and scarlet and most evenings they wore the brown skirts and black blouses which denoted that they belonged to the Youth League of National Uniformity and Pride, the NUAP as it was commonly known. They wore their NUAP uniforms on this particular morning as schools had been informed that the government would prefer as many pupils as possible to do this to emphasise and celebrate its third year of accession to power. Mr Ostanley was liberal with his own helping of cornflakes, he was taking part in a procession himself in the morning and he relished the thought of the afternoon. He asked his wife, who had become an excellent servant over the years, if she would prepare him a soft boiled egg. He sliced off the top and dug in his spoon. He fingered the papers in his inside jacket-pocket. Later, in the afternoon he was to serve them on Isobel Quirk. With luck, she could be in custody within a couple of days. The thought of this excited him and he did not notice the egg yolk dribble on his tie.

He had never liked her. He had expected confidences from her but had only received a most cool deference. She had been rude but her answers to some of his questions had left him feeling as though he had soiled his trousers. On their very first meeting he had exuded geniality only to be met by her damned put-downs.

'Ostanley, John Ostanley is the name. I'm looking forward to a long, involved relationship with you and your school. I have been in business for years so I know what makes the wheels click and what clogs them up. Any dirt in your machinery?'

He had winked as he had spoken, but Mrs Quirk had chosen to interpret this as a nervous tic. She had remained calm, too bloody calm, and had not smiled.

'I think that you will find that this school runs as smoothly as is possible without being harmful. The metaphor is a bit unfortunate as we are concerned with people rather than machines. The people here certainly manage to operate more than well without lubrication.'

She smiled now, he made the mistake of winking again.

'Come, come, you can say what you like to me. I know when to turn a blind eye.'

She had stood at this point though he was supposed to be doing the interviewing.

'Perhaps you would let me escort you about the school, keep both eyes open, there is plenty to see. I would hate you to miss anything.'

'Let's see your weakest teacher first. Every school carries its passengers, I want to see what I can do to lighten your load.'

'Were you ever a teacher?' she had retorted.

He looked at her alarmed, he had not come across this in the other schools he had visited. He had no quick answer, indeed she had given him little chance.

'I think it must be one of the most difficult of professions to make spot evaluations in. Instant judgments about what a teacher is or is not achieving are useless. What did you say your work was, Mr Ostanley?'

'I am an estate agent. I have two daughters of my own,' he had snapped as though his paternity qualified him to come to any educational conclusions which he sought to make. He stared at her coldly and added, 'Both are normal.'

'Aren't we all, Mr Ostanley? Normality is set by no rule or measuring tape. What appears normal to some, does not necessarily seem quite that to others. I'm sure your daughters are delightful girls. I'm sure that you will be interested in seeing our children, they are a very friendly bunch. Have you ever visited a school of this nature before?'

'No.'

'Then you will be surprised, I hope pleasantly surprised, by what we are able to achieve. We attempt to be a corporate staff, Mr Ostanley. There are no passengers here.'

'I see you're not a Party member.'

Isobel wore no arm-band.

'I have no affiliations save for the ones I have in this building — they are enough.'

'I would like to talk to all of your teachers individually. If you are — er — corporate, does that mean that you would prefer me not to do this?'

'On the contrary, Mr Ostanley, a school should be part of a reflection of a free society. Please feel free to talk with whoever you wish. There will be no hindrance or objection from me. Approach everyone in whatever way you want. You will need more than a half day of course, but come and visit us whenever you wish. Shall we visit the classrooms now?'

He had followed her round. The children seemed to have little or no respect for his bearing. His grey flannel suit, his official arm-band with the embroidered coat of arms on it all failed to impress them. They greeted him with smiles and much clutching and touching. He had been nauseated by it all. He had never seen children like them. Isobel noticed him recoil, as if he were forced to stroke a viper with its fangs drawn. Their friendly demonstrations of affection left him embarrassed. If they clung to his sleeve he unpeeled their fingers from him. He managed to pat the heads of a few of the least damaged and disturbed, usually as he was leaving a room. All he could find to say was 'Good, good.'

After scrutinising each teacher, he was anxious to leave each room.

'Odd-looking young woman that one,' he had remarked on Margaret Davis.

Isobel ignored the comment.

'How old is she?' he had asked of Madge Wragg.

'Young enough in spirit, Mr Ostanley.'

Isobel maintained a sweet formality. On reaching her room he had heaved a great forced sigh.

'I hadn't realised that such children existed.'

'They do more than that. They think and feel. Sometimes I believe their feelings and thoughts are more honest than ours. I have learned a great deal from them.'

'About your staff —'

'It's break-time in five minutes, do come into the staff room. You can meet all of them.' She continued to thwart him in this manner.

Instinctively he knew that the Prentice woman was the weak link. At first he thought that he might get somewhere with the deputy who looked like a retired cricketer. He had talked like one too — straight defensive bat and pecked at nothing on the off-side stump. The music teacher was a Jew

105

— no point in approaching him. He had to settle for Marjorie Prentice even though her heart was not in her betrayal; a prissy manner blessed with a silly tongue. He would use her, then dump her. The thought of dumping her caused him to smile as he entered her room for the first of their many *tête-à-têtes*, as Marjorie liked to call them. No wonder her husband had gone off with another woman.

'I've drawn a veil over that part of my life,' she had said. Ostanley pictured drawing the veil over her face and tightening it. When her talk was of no use that is what would be done with her. Veiled.

''Bye, Daddy,' his daughters chirped.

They pecked his cheek before leaving. He ordered another egg; he'd read the papers. He complained that the egg was too hard but finished it off. His wife saw him to the front step and waved. He had insisted that she repeat this each time he left the house. It was good for the neighbours to view how a decent family lived. He was always one for insisting on decent this, or decent that. It was his favourite word. Anything that was not decent was in decline. He did not consider Mrs Quirk or the wretched inmates of her school to be decent. In his brief-case he carried papers that would close it that very day. Her composure would crack a bit when this little bill of goods was delivered. How would she react to custody? Cheap heroics would not be allowed her way. The guardians had been well documented on the bitch. She wouldn't sound so clever today. As for her precious special care, they'd be special all right. So special that no one would ever have to look at them again. He switched the radio on as he climbed into his car. He liked a good brass band. Decent music, none of your namby-pamby stuff, something with a bit of pride in it. That's what he liked.

By the time he had reached the school the music had stirred him to dizzying heights of self-importance and grandeur. He was met in the foyer by the school-keeper who approached him apologetically.

'We weren't expecting you until this afternoon, sir. I suppose you've come about the situation?'

He spread his hands out to signify a physical question. Ostanley did not understand the implication of his gestures.

'What situation? What do you know about it?'

'No more than you do, sir. It's come as a surprise to me. I don't know what's going on. None of the parents have telephoned in. It's not a holiday is it?'

It was then that Ostanley noticed the unusual quietness within the building. A school void of children had the same hollow quality of some of the empty houses he had sold. They were always easier to sell if people were in them. Once vacant they lost their human smell, the odour of an empty house always gave it sinister overtones. Ostanley sniffed. Nothing stirred. He banged violently on the door to Isobel's study, he thumped it hard with his fist demanding some kind of answer.

'The door isn't locked, sir. There's no one in.'

Ostanley jammed down the handle and flung the door back so that it crashed hard against the wall.

Unopened letters were stacked neatly on her desk. Her armchair was vacant, the four other chairs which surrounded the long low coffee table were all dusted, clean, but empty. The rocking-horse, which on all the other occasions when he had visited had been in motion, was quite still. No child jockey sat astride it. He kicked it hard, so that it spun across the room and crashed against the glass-sided cupboard. The glass splintered but did not break. His rage and anger was still not abated. He tore the children's paintings from their moorings on the wall, screwed the words into balls of paper or tore them into shreds before hurling them into the direction of the paper bin. He banged on her desk with his fist and stamped his foot on the carpet until his ankle pained him. He turned to the school-keeper who stood in the open doorway, a silent witness to his petulance and rage.

'Don't just bloody well stand there,' Ostanley roared at him.

The school-keeper barely smothered his contempt for the older man's tantrums.

'What did you want me to do, sir? Shall I begin clearing up the mess now?' He glanced about the study.

'Where the hell are they?' Ostanley held up his hands as if he were going to seize the lapels of the keeper's jacket. The keeper stood his ground and looked at the hands. They were shaking. He side-stepped Ostanley and placed the rocking-horse in its correct position. He picked up the pens and crayons that had fallen from the desk. He scrutinised the cracked glass.

'I don't know where they are. I'm doing my job. You do yours, all of this has nothing to do with me. Did you want to use the telephone?'

The receiver had bounced off its base. The school-keeper put it to his ear and then replaced it.

'It's still working, sir,' he said and continued with his insolent tidying.

Ostanley sat in one of the chairs, he needed time, he was frightened. The guardians were not over-pleased with the way the Prentice woman had gone. It had required police co-operation to cover it all up. Misadventure or accidental death was to be recorded. She had tripped on the stairs, fallen and broken her neck. Ostanley had suggested that they might infer alcoholism. He had been called a fool by the Director of Internal Security. He had been warned to tread carefully. He had now begun to realise that uniformity required a pathway which became increasingly more narrow. If things went wrong someone had to be blamed. His position had become most uncomfortable, today was not going to progress according to plan.

'Do you want to use the telephone, sir?'

The school-keeper stood there with a dustpan and brush in his hand.

'No, get out. Mrs Quirk should have informed me if she was taking part in the procession. I've no objections, it's an excellent idea, but she should have let me know.'

108

'They're not taking part in any —'

'Get out.'

The school-keeper closed the door. Ostanley sat himself in her chair. He would see her tomorrow, all thoughts of the procession sickened him. He would maintain that she had informed him that she was closing the school for that purpose and that he had agreed to the closure.

A good business always ran itself, money made money, and Ostanley's business was strictly hierarchial in nature so that it had reached the point where his underlings could earn him enough money without him bothering to have to do much except check up on things for two hours each day. He would escape to his own office, miss the procession. Where had the rotten cow gone? He half-waved to the school-keeper to signify that he was leaving. At the entrance of the school gates two mothers blocked his exit with their prams. He waited for one of them to pull a pram away. They carried on talking, he had to speak to them.

'Can I come past? Would you mind?'

The fattest of the two women who had a large shopping bag hanging on her arm withdrew her pram. She tilted her head on one side and gave him an indifferent stare. If he had felt better he would have given her a mouthful. As he brushed past the pram, she pushed the hood down. It was empty. He hurried past her.

'I know he will be safe if he is with her.'

The fat woman's words made his ears burn and it took a great deal of effort to put the ignition key into its place. He was glad to be able to place his hands on the steering wheel, they had begun to shake again.

13

'That's one hundred,' Margaret relinquished the balloon gently from her grasp and watched it wobble in the air before it sailed silently away from the attic window. Fortunately the conditions for such an operation were perfect. The day had begun warm and just now a slight breeze filtered through the sun's morning haze. Margaret turned in a dreamlike fashion that befitted her occupation and chose a yellow balloon from the cardboard box and slipped the lip of the balloon on the end of the helium gas container. Leslie turned the handle of the gas tap. Margaret watched and felt the rubber swell and rise as it was inflated, it was a pleasant sensation. At a nod from Leslie, she tied the lip of the balloon with great dexterity and then quickly attached a labelled message. She released it as gently as she would have freed an imprisoned dove.

'You're a dab hand at this, I can hardly keep up with you,' Leslie admired her skill and swiftness.

'I did something like this years ago, before I began teaching. I worked in a sausage factory for a day, just one day. All I had to do was slip the skin over the edge of this spout-ended machine. We made them in all shapes and sizes. The sausage meat kept chugging out. I had to keep slipping the skins on or I would have got an eyeful.'

'Sexy.'

'Leslie! Please. I wasn't really doing the job, I was doing some modelling work for some rubber gloves — but I felt I ought to know what it was all about. My hands came out in a rash afterwards.' She looked at her hands. 'You never know when a skill might become useful. I have never eaten sausages since that day.'

She let another balloon drift into the air.

Leslie had worked out that a certain amount of gas with some extra weight added to the tailing message would result in most of the balloons landing in or round London or its immediate suburbs. There was no sense in floating the balloons into the sea. They worked silently for the most part but after Margaret had released 500 she paused for a rest. She sat with her elbows resting on the window-ledge and gazed at the coloured dots peppering the sky.

'They look lovely.'

'Yes they do,' Leslie agreed.

'Everything is well so far, they don't even know we are here. I mean the guardians.' She laughed.

'They do know the telephone has been cut off,' Leslie sighed.

'It's been out of order since ten, so someone knows. My transmitter has been sabotaged by crackle, it can't be interference from the weather. I managed to get some messages through, though.'

'Who to?'

'Anyone who was listening, we have to take all risks and all chances.'

'Perhaps it was someone you spoke to who has informed.'

111

'Highly likely, but there was no alternative. I got three hours of messages in.'

He yawned, Margaret could see that he was weary. He detected her thoughts.

'Let's get on with this,' he said.

'It's better if all of them land before dusk. Do you need a break?'

'No.'

'Come on then.'

She ignored the rough edge to his voice. He never spoke like that to Isobel. Margaret was not hurt, she understood these things. Another balloon floated away.

Over the years, the numbers at the community of Holy Compassion had dwindled. The order had been in existence for twenty years or more and served as a bastion of a contemplative order. At the height of its devotions there had been fifteen brothers in the house and the adjoining chapel. There were now only three members left, Father Thomas, and Brothers Matthew and James. They lived frugally and, apart from a meagre grant from the main clerical authorities, eked a subsistence from their gardening and a few hens. For most of the time they were near starvation. In spite of the rather forgotten nature of their being, they continued to pray diligently.

In the past, the monks had left their labours and gathered together in the small chapel for prayer. However, although the programme of worship was still strictly adhered to in the present situation, in order to conserve their strength, they had been forced to absolve themselves from many of the corporate gatherings and to pray where they were at the time. Father Thomas looked at his watch and rang the hand-bell which he carried about with him and then knelt to pray in the spinach patch. His back ached and his knees creaked at the joints. His arthritis crept slowly over his body and, try as he might, he found the pain difficult to ignore. He closed his eyes and began his prayers. The pain in his back and knee-joints caused his head to throb. The sun was particularly warm, his shaven pate was most vulnerable. He felt nauseous and dizzy and before his devotions were a quarter over he had toppled forward and lay sprawled face down in the spinach. The wetness of the plants revived him, he lay there and opened his eyes. Was it death? Had his Maker finally called him? The spinach was still there. Yet he felt very strange. Half-conscious from his swoon he lay for a while spread-eagled as though in some act of total subjugation and adoration. He did not wish to convey alarm to the other two brothers. He ought really to make an attempt to finish off his prayers yet the effort of moving seemed beyond him. He was about to close his eyes once more and then blinked. The balloon came to his notice.

Normally, he would have ignored such worldly frippery and probably regarded it as an unnecessary intrusion into the order's chosen closed pattern of existence. The red balloon gently bounced and bobbed among the spinach before momentarily settling itself an inch or two from his nose. He went to grasp it. Not being used to the handling of such an object, he touched the top of its shiny surface with his hand. It evaded his grasp and floated from him; he felt thwarted. He lunged at it, catching its side with the edge of his finger-nail. The bang shocked him from his trance-like state and dispelled any thoughts that he might be about to levitate from his mind. He sat up and contemplated the shrivelled rubber which lay among the leaves. He picked it up and found the note attached to its lip. He opened it.

'God bless you.

My name is Pauline Bontil and I feel it is my duty to ask your assistance in the name of the Father, the Son, the Holy Ghost and the blessed Virgin Mary. We have twelve children in our care whose lives are threatened by the State. If you believe, as I do, that human life is sacred, then please demonstrate or make yourselves known outside the enclosed address.

113

All the children are wounded and maimed but for that matter so was our Lord. Please make yourself known on and for our behalf and oppose Section 138 of the Code of Common Conformity. The enactment of this section means death for the children in our care. Help us protect them. Pray for us, bear witness for us. The blessing of the Trinity is with you — be with us. Pauline Mary Bontil, Teacher.'

Father Thomas carefully folded the note and slipped it safely into his cassock pocket. He had little difficulty in completing his prayers, his head was clear and he accepted the pain in his joints. When his devotions were over he picked enough spinach to fill his appended scapular and he carried the plants in it as though it were an apron. Even so, when boiled the quantity shrank.

A plate of watery spinach topped with a poached egg and subsidised by one slice of bread provided the brothers with their main meal of the day. Apart from the hour taken for lunch, the brothers observed contemplative silence throughout the day. Even when the order was at its height in numbers the hour where talk was allowed did not reverberate with conversational cut and thrust. Even when the order had postulants and novices, there was little chatter. The tradition had continued, indeed it had become more intensified. As in everything but prayer, a strict economy was practised. Words were no exception. The three brothers dipped their bread and ate slowly, their combined ages totalled 184 years. They had little to say to each other, gossip was unknown to them and meal times were now usually as silent as the rest of the day. Bodily aches and pains were borne and not discussed, and as the Father Superior, Father Thomas, never mentioned his debility, neither did the other two brothers. The encroaching years did not allow them to be plaintive about the ravaging effects that time had upon their bodies. Their souls remained intact.

Father Thomas waited until Brother James had finished mopping up the last of his food before he passed the note

114

across the table. He made no comment on its content but waited for some reaction from his compatriots. They both read the letter. It was Brother Mathew who spoke first.

'We should do something.'

'Pray,' Brother James intervened.

'I agree ...' Father Thomas faltered and Brother Matthew recognised that his superior was unsure, he wanted suggestions from them, not mere obedience. Having placed the art of conversation in abeyance for most of their lives, they now found it difficult to string a few words together, it was alien for them to orchestrate phrases. The words had to be torn from their vocal chords. Brother Matthew moved his lips but no sounds were uttered, the lips trembled. Brother James swallowed hard and burped, he was troubled by an ulcer. He nodded his head again and again. Father Thomas was forced to lead a discussion. It was an incredible event.

'It seems that the days of the existence of this order are limited to the time that we three have left to spend on this earth. The Bishop has made it quite clear that no more postulants will come our way. Our numbers can never grow. However, I do not believe that our time has been wasted or mis-spent. Yet this note, which came into my hands in the most strange manner, has ruptured my complacency, or rather it has presented me with a sense of urgency with regard to something which is happening in the world beyond these cloisters. You are both now aware of the contents of the letter. I know that its content is not an exaggeration. I have prayed, yet the usual balm has not entered my being. I feel the need, I feel that we, as a community have been called to do something different, something special. Perhaps, yes perhaps, something that is holy. As yet, I do not know what we should do.' He clasped his knobbled hands together and looked at his companions directly. Eyes were averted on normal occasions.

'Pray,' said Brother James.

'It is all that we can do.' said Brother Matthew.

115

'Yes,' Father Thomas sighed deeply.

They sat in silence. Then Father Thomas smiled, it was a long, slow smile of enlightenment.

'Brothers, my dear brethren, you are right. We must pray. But the question we must ask ourselves is ... where? In what place should we pray? I think that we should contemplate whether or not we should sacrifice our own needs, our own comforts. What would you say is our greatest comfort?'

'The Lord Jesus.' Brother James was in no doubt and Brother Matthew rapidly agreed.

'He will remain with us as He is now.' Father Thomas stood up and tapped the wall over the fire-place. Fragments of loose plaster fell to the ground.

'It's this decaying building that is our refuge, our comfort, our shelter. How would we fare without the building? After we are gone, what does it become? None of us are young, all of us are at peace with our Maker. Do we need the building? Would it be ...' He paused, and returned to his seat. He rested his elbows on the table and propped his head on clasped hands.

'Would it be a disobedient gesture if we left it?'

'Leave here?' Brother James was startled.

'Where would we go?' Brother Matthew asked unhopefully.

'God moves mysteriously, he guides us accordingly. It is my belief that this shows us our pathway.' He held up the note. 'We should pray, of that I am in no doubt. But, we should offer our succour in the form of prayer inside this building, or outside of it.' He pointed to the address on the note. 'It will require great effort on our part, it may mean that we will have to brave the cold evenings. Our bodies are not strong but our souls brothers ... what of them? Would they carry us through a testing ordeal of silent witness? A witness of sanctity for the poor and maimed? Can we allow ourselves to be cossetted and prevented from doing what we should do by remaining here? Think of our Lord, what would

116

He have done? I suggest we retire for prayer and seek some guidance from Him. I have opened my thoughts to you. God bless us and give us enlightenment. We will speak more of this matter at the same time tomorrow.'

Father Thomas muttered thanks for their repast and they left for their cells, where all three prayed with fresh vigour and diligence.

Miriam Heldman and Ruby Theberton had been neighbours for twenty years. Their gardens were separated by a fence that was little more than 2 feet high. These gardens bore witness to the fact that the two women shared things. Premature widowhood had hit them both. Ruby's husband had died from a protracted illness of bowel cancer and two weeks later Miriam's husband had had a stroke at work and died from a cerebral haemorrhage. His departure had been swift. In their solitary years they still argued with one another but the arguments were merely a throw-back to the times when both women had served on the local council representing opposite sides of the two main political parties of the day. Miriam was a lifetime Socialist and Ruby had been born into Conservatism in a grocer's shop in Cheam. In their different ways both ladies had cared deeply for the communities that they had been elected to serve. The power of decisions had see-sawed every three years or so and both women had sat in ruling or opposite seats. They had come to respect and like each other in spite of their differing ideals. Both were shocked when they were jointly ousted from office by the National Uniformity Group. They almost experienced a double bereavement when they were informed that they could not stand for re-election again. If there were no elections, how could they?

'There's a bit of larkspur here, Miriam, the last lot I gave you hasn't taken. Give it plenty of water, dear, when you dig it in, they need a lot of water to start them off.' Ruby handed Miriam a large root. 'Look how well the Golden Rain has come up, I never expected so much of it, it spreads quickly doesn't it? We'll have to curb it in the same way as the lily of the valley. It seems a shame to chuck plants out.'

As neither woman could find it in her heart to throw away plants, their gardens had become identical in growth. Fortunately, the planning of each was slightly different. Their gardens, like their politics, were democratic without being quite the same, the ingredients were just planted in different places. The total effect had an *ad hoc* charm that was not unpleasing.

'I've put the kettle on, it'll whistle us when it's ready, shall I come your side or will you come mine?' Miriam asked.

'It's my turn today, I was over your side yesterday. I'll get the cups and milk ready, bring the teapot over, we can sit in the deck-chairs.'

The kettle had begun to wail, Miriam placed the larkspur root in a bucket of water, returned to the house, washed her hands and brewed the tea. The sun was hot and the women talked less than usual. Yesterday they had talked of nationalising the banks and Ruby had called Miriam a Communist. She had called her such names before, but always retracted later.

'We'll never see eye to eye Miriam but heart to heart is a different matter.'

It was too warm, too hot for a good old humdinger of an argument today, they often repeated themselves anyway and the net result was usually a draw. The present disillusionment among the populace dismayed them and both agreed that the proletariat had become lumpen. There was always a bit of ginger about in the good old days. But now, there was no point in questioning anything. Ruby poured out the tea and Miriam fanned herself with the newspaper.

'It's all it's bloody good for, I could write a better newspaper than this.'

'No private enterprise, that's what happens,' said Ruby.

'It's not the point I was making,' Miriam continued to fan

118

herself as Ruby passed the cup to her. They sipped in silence and paid little heed to the greenfly which seemed intent on causing them some irritation. Their separate thoughts provided immunity.

'We'll win a prize if it lands on us,' Ruby stared intently into the sky.

'What?' Miriam continued to fan herself, her view obscured by the newspaper.

'The balloon, look, see it's just bounced off the roof at the bottom. With luck it will be ours. Mrs Simpson won 2 pounds of tea like that last year. Do you see it, it's blue?' Ruby pointed to the balloon and Miriam let the newspaper drop from her hand on the lawn.

'Mrs Simpson would win 2 pounds of tea, she would win it.'

'If she won it fair and square, Miriam, I don't see how you can quibble.'

Ruby stood up and shaded her eyes by putting her hand to her brow.

'The tailpiece will get caught on the laburnum tree, look, Miriam, it gives you the address in the tail piece. It's entangled, it's ours. Come on my girl where's your initiative we might win up to £50. You never know.'

Miriam stood up, now grudgingly curious. A bit of extra cash wouldn't go amiss.

'You keep an eye on it, I'll get the step-ladder, you don't want to hurt yourself,' she said.

Miriam placed the ladder in position; she did the climbing as Ruby was prone to high blood pressure and heights made her dizzy. Miriam managed to disentangle the balloon without much bother while Ruby held the steps steady.

'Take the note off the bottom,' Ruby called up.

'Wait a minute, hold your horses, let me get down first. Do you want me to break my bloody neck?'

'Miriam,' Ruby had always disapproved of Miriam's swearing.

She hadn't realised that Jews swore anyway. However, Miriam was a different kind of Jew because she didn't believe and had married a Gentile. She and her husband had both been members of the same trade union. Ruby had always thought both of them to be common. She still thought that Miriam was common but it didn't stop her regarding the woman as her best friend. She trusted Miriam.

Miriam untied the note and let the balloon bob away.

'You should have kept it, what a shame to let it go.' Ruby spoke in false pique.

'Don't be silly. What in God's name would you have done with that object?'

Ruby nodded her head in agreement, but she watched the balloon bob away over the next two gardens. As a lifetime Conservative she had never been mean, but just couldn't abide waste.

'Some child will find it,' said Miriam.

Ruby took comfort from the thought. Miriam had opened the note.

'Well? What have we won?' asked Ruby. Miriam had read the note but had not passed it to her.

'Nothing,' said Miriam. She handed the note to Ruby and picked up the newspaper and began to fan herself once more.

Ruby read the note aloud.

'To whom it may concern.

My name is Margaret Davis. I am a teacher. I wonder if you would kindly give some thought to the plight of a few children placed in the care of my school? Please do not crumble this note up if you think that I am begging for money for school funds. Please read on.'

'A bit bossy isn't she,' said Ruby.

'Read on, girl, read on,' Miriam added testily as she swotted a few greenfly away from her fleshy arm.

'Our school used to cater for children who were both mentally and physically handicapped. The most extreme cases were/are called special-care children. Under the new Code of

Conformity Section 138, the present government seeks to "tranquillise these persons out of existence." Put bluntly this means that the children who are most dear, most precious, most special to us are to be put to death. As a staff we could not allow this and have chosen to disobey this section of the code. We have the children with us at the address given below. We have taken our stance not out of any measure of obstinacy or disrespect for law or order. We believe that no one has the right to kill or take away life in this way. Perhaps you are not aware of Section 138. It has been given little reportage. Help us stop it being further enacted. If you could see our children you would understand our feelings. I am asking you to declare your feelings about this matter. How you do this is your concern. Please help us to protect our children. Lots of love to you from them and me. Margaret Davis, Class Teacher.'

'Oh dear, we haven't won anything. Do you think it's all true?' Ruby was discomfited and upset by the contents of the note. The afternoon was ruined.

'Of course it's true, it never could have happened in our day, Ruby. The worst of both sides couldn't have concocted up anything as vicious as this. They are a set of right bastards. Everything they do, they say they do because it is right.'

Miriam paused and sipped her tea, she placed her hand on Ruby's forearm.

'There's no love in them, Ruby, no caring, it's all gone.' Miriam began to sniffle.

'Stop that noise, Miriam, stop it. We have to think. At last we have something to do.'

Miriam stopped, she hadn't heard Ruby talk like that since their council chamber days. She was a true battle-axe when something got her going. Miriam straightened herself up and adjusted the deck-chair into a less languorous position.

'We should do something, you are quite right.'

Miriam dabbed her eyes dry.

'We mustn't break the law,' said Ruby.

121

Miriam made a snorting sound and found her electioneering tongue once again.

'Break the law, break the law. It's damned difficult not to break it these days, there are new laws going through by the minute. I wonder if we should have even read the note, or whether the balloon had a right to straddle our laburnum tree. At the rate things are going on we'll be having to fill in a form before we take a shit.'

'Miriam!' Ruby interrupted, but Miriam was in full throttle.

'It is her Jewish blood coming through again,' thought Ruby. Although Miriam ate pork and practised no religion, Ruby tended to blame her small foibles and histrionics on her blood. Miriam had lived as a Gentile.

'It's true, Ruby, and what's more you know it. The police go along with all that they are asked to do.'

'They have to, dear, that's why they are the police,' Ruby consoled.

'Imagine, no, you don't have to imagine. In ten or fifteen years they'll knock at our door. Yours and mine. They'll knock on the door with a slip of paper and then cart us off. God alone knows where.'

'Oh, Miriam, perish the thought.'

'It's not a thought. It's a reality. What are we going to do about this?'

'I think we should stand outside the place.'

'Demonstrate,' said Miriam her eyes glistening with anticipation.

'If you want to put it that way dear, but we should persuade. That's how our votes were won. Persuasion, that's what is needed. That's what will count. I don't want to break the law, no never. Arthur wouldn't have wanted that, God rest him, but he would expect me to stand up and be counted on a matter of principle. He was like that about the National Anthem, you know.'

'Yes, I know, dear,' Miriam dryly added.

'If I can find three people to join me and you can do the

same there will be six in all. We can picket the front of the house.'

Ruby looked alarmed when she heard this. 'Not me. Picketing! You know I've always been against that.'

'Well all right we could pers-u-a-de in front of the house. Just think of it as selling paper flags for charities the way you used to,' Miriam cajoled.

'Oh, that would be nice, the girls will love it. I can wear my blue hat. I haven't worn it for years. Do you think I should take the feather off it? You don't see so many around nowadays.'

'What?'

'Feathers on hats.'

'Keep it on, you look stylish in it and it makes you look taller. We'll begin tomorrow midday.'

Miriam got up from the deck-chair. She loathed the present political regime; Ruby was constantly appalled and sickened by its assaults on individuality and for the first time the two women achieved some kind of mystical political unity.

'It will be just like the war years again,' Ruby spoke with nostalgia.

'I'll help you in with the tea things, then we have some telephoning to do,' said Miriam.

All the messages did not meet with such heights in debate or soul-searching. Most of them received a resoundingly tepid reception. The majority of people did not search their consciences or look for any recesses of compassion that might have been untapped for months or even years. For the most part they wallowed in their complacency. They kept the balloons and threw the messages away, usually without comment. A minority informed the guardian police. However, there were some who were motivated to do something, to picket, to persuade, to make known their disapproval. The affiliations of these groups of people were as dispersed as late summer poppy-seeds, and far too numerous and varied

123

to mention. Some supporters did exist though, and for different reasons chose to demonstrate that they cared.

At the house in Bayswater the company gathered for their evening meal. So far everything had gone according to plan. The adults had found a deeper respect between themselves, friendships had strengthened, love was corporate, and in some sections even latent passions had been aroused. They sat for their evening meal and not one of them could deny that the present offered them a finer state of happiness that they had not known for years. Whether they realised it or not they had reason to thank the children within their care for their own present state of bliss.

14

'Don't lift all those, Madge, leave them for me to carry over,' Harry Wintner was referring to the large stack of plates which Madge was about to lift from the table over to the sink. She declined his offer of help firmly but sweetly.

'Carry on with what you are doing, I'm not too proud to ask for assistance if I need it.'

'There.' She placed the plates in the soapy water and took up a tea-towel.

'I'll fill the kettle, we need some more hot water. We must save the other for bathing the children.' She placed the large copper kettle under the tap and turned it. Coughing and spluttering noises came from the spout of the tap and a few dribbles of water spottled through. Then nothing.

'Damn, something's gone wrong, it must be an air lock,' she said.

Harry shook his head sadly. Madge raised a pencilled eyebrow questioningly.

'It's started. They've begun their attack,' he spoke quietly.

'Attack?' Madge dipped her forefinger and tested the temperature of the washing-up water that was available. She shook her head, the water was less than tepid.

'They've cut off our water supplies.' Harry wiped his hands dry as he spoke.

'The bastards, we're done for.' Madge took the towel from him and swiped at imaginary mosquitoes as though to exorcise the enemy. With an abruptness that shocked Harry, she buried her face in the towel. The prospect of such a sudden defeat was too much for her. She groaned into the cloth.

'Don't worry, old girl, don't worry,' he placed his arm round her shoulder, stroked the fine strands of hair and then lightly kissed the back of her neck. Madge dropped the towel on the floor and straightened up. He took both her hands, squeezed them gently and chuckled. 'We've got water, enough to last us a lifetime.'

'What?'

'We have a well. It's in the cellar. Reuben has tested the water. It's in better nick than any of this stuff.' He turned on the useless tap.

'The fetching and carrying will just mean a bit more work, that's all.'

'Oh, Harry,' she threw her arms about him and the elderly couple clasped each other together with joy and relief.

Nothing shocked Isobel. She stood in the entrance of the kitchen doorway and waited until they had untwined before she spoke. Isobel could not tell whether or not Madge's technicoloured complexion had blushed. Harry did not seem remotely embarrassed. He spoke first.

'I suppose you've come about the water?'

'Yes.' Isobel entered the kitchen and merged with the ritual of stacking plates away. It was easier to talk while one was working.

126

'Reuben has five water-barrels. He has decided to place them in strategic positions. He and Shirley will see to it that they are never empty. I came to tell you that one will be placed in here. Bathing among adults has to be restricted.'

'That's no problem, people bath too much nowadays. A good wipe over and a bit of scent does just as well,' said Madge.

Harry nodded.

'Everything all right then?' Isobel placed the last of the plates in position.

'Fine, fine,' the couple chorused.

Shirley let her fingers drift lightly over the box of hand-grenades. She took one from the box and felt its weight, she enjoyed the feel of the metal and found the formal design of squares attractive to look at. The oval heavyweight fitted into the palm of her hand. Her eyes beseeched the small pin. Her life had been full of explosions of one kind or another. The thought of a real explosion, the shock, the violence of it, the bang, the debris flying, thrilled and excited her. She knew that this was wrong, morally wrong and that it was con-nected with the passions that had always ruled her life. At one time she had felt that she had cured herself of these destructive impulses. Her marriage had been good, she had felt comfortable, secure, particularly in the early years. She had worked to make it so. She had never come to terms with her husband's betrayal. The betrayal had brought back the old fierceness, the old scratching at her innards had returned. Shirley wanted to fight.

'Put it down, they must be handled with care. It says so on the box,' said Reuben.

'I'm handling it carefully.'

'Lovingly, I would say. It's not good for you.' Reuben dis-liked the expression on Shirley's face. He took the grenade from her and placed it carefully back in its former position in the box. 'It could explode ...' he took both her upper arms in his hands, 'it could explode with just a caress.'

'Like you, Reuben, just like you. You're like a hand-grenade.'

Reuben cut her chortling short.

'No, that is not true. I would not explode if I didn't want to. The grenade has no choice, it is entirely in your hands. I am not.'

He pulled her to him and kissed her long and hard. He licked her throat and gently nibbled at her ears savouring her face slowly. He stopped abruptly and held her away from him. She was breathless and shocked.

'We are here to defend, not to attack. If you require my love remember that.'

'Require your love?' Shirley spoke in an exasperated manner, half-mockingly. 'We both required, r-e-quired,' she repeated the word. 'We both required sex, Reuben, so we are having it.'

'If that is all it is then I shall withdraw it. I can meet that requirement alone. I had done so for years before I shared it with you.'

She slapped him hard on the face. He returned the gesture almost spontaneously; her head jerked back. Both faced each other with the box of grenades snuggled at their sides.

'You require love,' he said.

She nodded and followed him submissively out of the armaments room into the last of the cellars until they reached the edge of the well.

'I'm sorry I struck you,' he said.

'You were defending. I'm not sorry,' Shirley's jaw still burned from the impact of the blow but her innards were calm. Shirley Merchant could not believe her luck, she was being loved. It was more than she had bargained for. She sighed with contentment and peered into the well.

'Leslie made this,' Reuben pointed to the winch-wheel which straddled the aperture of the well. The wheel held four buckets. 'It works on the same principle as the old water-wheel except that the bars stop the buckets from emptying

128

their contents once they are full. We will feel the weight when all four buckets are full. It will be impossible to turn the handle in reverse. Afterwards, we wind them up with the other handle. Like this, so,' he demonstrated.

Shirley was a little perturbed by the suddenness of his practicality of tone. She complained.

'Why are you telling me all this? I'm not a bloody engineer.'

Reuben remained calm and continued to wind the handle of the winch. The four buckets brimming with water were brought up to the lip of the well. He set the handle-lock on the winch.

'There,' he smiled and directed Shirley's glare to the buckets.

'You may be working it alone sometimes, or with someone else. We can't always be working together. If the water is needed and I am not available or not here even — do you want to be inadequate or obsolete?'

She did not answer his questions but he could see that her frown had softened and almost disappeared. He cupped his hands together and held some water in them.

'Here, taste, taste,' he said. She drank.

'It's very cold, very good,' she said. She finished slurping it from his hands and then licked his palms. He did not take his hands away, she continued to lick both his palms. He withdrew both his hands.

'I'm a bitch, Reuben, aren't I?'

'No, not always. Come, Lassie, help me fill the barrels. You can wind up the next few gallons.'

'I'm enjoying my training.'

'I'll reward you sweetly when you please me,' he said.

Once more Shirley entered a submissive tranquil state of being, perhaps Reuben knew that this was what she sought of him. The extent of his control seemed to know no bounds. Shirley grunted and turned the wheel so that the water could flow. Reuben let her get on with it; both were satisfied.

'Do you hear it?' Pauline pushed open the window of the attic to its limit and leaned half her body out.

'Be careful, dear,' said Beryl, laying a restraining hand on Pauline's shoulder.

'I can hear the singing, they're not young voices. Is it the three old men?'

Leslie was helping mend a broken cot-rail. He looked up from his screwdriver.

'I have binoculars. They arrived an hour ago. They are monks or priests or something like that. They were kneeling outside the front gate. You can see them from the other window. I think that they are our first supporters. I'm worried for them, they look a bit frail to me.'

'It's a vigil, they will stay there while the children are here.' Pauline's eyes filled with tears. She turned once more and stretched out of the window anxious to hear the voices; the sound was more distinct now, the noise of the traffic had abated.

'O Blest Creator of the light
Who makest the day with radiance bright
And o'er the forming world didst call
The light from chaos first of all.'

'It's beautiful, quite beautiful. They must have received one of your messages, Pauline.'

Pauline sat on the window-ledge elated with the knowledge. Leslie had finished mending the cot, and waited until the singing ceased before he chose to speak. Beryl busied herself re-tucking in the edges of the blankets round each bed.

'How long do you think they will stay, Pauline? They are hardly clothed for a whole evening. We could be here for days. One of them might peg out if they stay there all night.' Leslie was genuinely concerned for the well-being of the aged men.

'They'll stay all night and the next, and the next. They will stay until our situation is resolved. They are supporting in the only way they know. It's for themselves; they will hope, no pray, for succour. If it comes their way, they will accept it. If it does not, they will still be undeterred.'

'Succour? They'll need blankets if they are thinking of staying there tonight.'

Leslie tapped the top of the cot with his screwdriver as if to ratify his handiwork as well as his observations. Beryl paused and looked up from the last of the beds, Leslie's way of saying things could, at times, be construed as being banal or facetious. He was neither. She took him seriously.

'We have spare blankets here, double large blankets that are surplus to our needs. It would be quite simple to make a hole in the centre of three of them, but how do we deliver them?'

'What does each blanket need a hole for?' asked Pauline. The singing had stopped and she had closed the window.

'They could slip their heads through the holes and wrap the blankets round them. You have seen them in geography books, they are called *gauchos*.'

'Ponchos,' Leslie corrected.

'Oh, what a marvellous idea, Beryl.' Pauline looked across the lawn. 'But how on earth are we to get them out to them? It's a bit like being in a lighthouse.'

'Reuben and Shirley will deliver them, they know the safe route,' said Leslie.

'But, Shirley, doesn't believe, she never has and —'

Leslie did not let Pauline finish.

'Shirley will abide by our decisions. Isobel would not seek to disbar anyone from supporting us. Nor would she stop us offering them a little —'

'Succour,' said Pauline.

'A little bit of that; Reuben and Shirley will not object. They will deliver the goods when it is a little darker.'

Pauline was pleased with Leslie's assurances; she joined Beryl and the two of them sat together in the aisle between the cots and beds. Some of the children had begun to grunt and gurgle, others made odd sounds which might have represented words. Leslie made his way from the cot he had mended and was about to go to consult Isobel. He could hear tapping. An incessant rhythm which got steadily louder. Beryl detected the concern in his expression.

'Don't worry, it's Margaret,' she said.

He raised his eyebrows.

'She's going to tap-dance for the children; we usually sing to them before they go to sleep, but we felt a little dance would make a nice change. I love Margaret.'

Pauline's simplicity was not contrived. Leslie scratched his head as Margaret came into the room. Pauline and Beryl clapped and the children mirrored their applause by making sounds of joy and appreciation.

'Where the hell had she got all that gear from?' Leslie wondered.

Margaret was dressed like a cinema usherette of the mid-1940s. She wore a white blouse with a black bow-tie; the blouse was encased tightly within a maroon waistcoat which fitted her as though it had been pasted on.

'It's a good job she has a blouse on,' thought Leslie, 'otherwise her tits might pop right over the top of the waistcoat.'

That part of Margaret's anatomy did seem to have been pushed higher than normal. The rigours of the uniform demanded it this way. Her maroon skirt just covered her pink satin knickers so that plenty of black-stockinged leg was left for the eye of the beholder. On her feet were a pair of red tap-dancing shoes with black bows.

'I got it after doing a cigarette advert years ago. They wouldn't let me dance then, of course. I just sold cancer to millions. They're tap-shoes I've had since I was seventeen.' Margaret pointed to them.

'Heirlooms,' said Leslie.

Margaret ignored him. If he didn't want to watch her dance, then no one was stopping him from leaving.

'Which one would you like? Oh, I know one that we'll all like. It has a lovely chorus. Off we go, then.'

Margaret sang and tapped her way up and down the aisle. She would flip her feet, wave her arms and tilt her behind as the rhythm demanded. Pauline was transfixed and Beryl and Leslie watched gleefully.

'I'm looking over a four-leafed clover
That I overlooked before,
Sometimes it's sunshine, and sometimes it's rain
Sometimes ...'

Margaret completed her act by doing the splits. Beryl winced at the thought' of doing such a thing, Pauline gasped in amazement and Leslie wondered if she had damaged her fanny permanently. She confounded them all by leaping onto the points of her toes and taking a swift bow. Applause, applause from all quarters. Margaret then clapped her hands.

'Quiet times now, quiet times now,' she demanded of the children.

Pauline and Beryl began to flit from bed to bed making each child comfortable for the night. Margaret had begun to croon 'Now the day is over' and Leslie felt it was time to see Isobel.

'I enjoyed that,' he whispered into Margaret's ear as he passed her.

She nodded thanks but kept singing 'Shadows of the evening drift across the sky'.

Isobel's diary had never reflected the internal impressions that the day had made upon her. During her years at school it was full of staccato comments and reminders of things that she had to do. When viewed in retrospect some of the matters seemed miniscule, humdrum, inane, hardly worth noting. Yet at the time the details that they encompassed were imperative. She glanced at the sheet before her. Check amounts of dried milk. More relief for Pauline and Beryl (I must be with them during the afternoon). Could people presently involved with defence strategies offer help to Madge and Harry? Review this situation. Reduce pheno-barb dose for Timothy and ask Beryl to time the length of his fits. See Reuben and Shirley about water distribution. The telephone is dead and the water is cut off. We have begun our strategies: water is available, communication with the outside is restricted, but we have made some contact. Resolve has not weakened individually or collectively.

In spite of the items in her diary, Isobel found herself making a futile attempt to run a bath ten minutes after writing it. As soon as the tap coughed she realised her mistake. It had been the same at school, fatigue always manifested itself in vagueness or forgetfulness; she was rarely irritable. Nevertheless, she was annoyed and angry with herself for ceding to it and finding herself in a room attempting to do something which was futile and wasteful. She hurried from it and took a bowl from where they were stacked near the sink. She then filled it from the water butt which was placed on the landing. A warm bath before retiring had always helped Isobel profoundly, she would miss it. She carried the bowl of water into her room.

The cold water made her gasp. She had stripped herself naked and was wiping herself all over with a wet cloth. At first, she let the water dribble slowly between her breasts and down towards her navel. She shuddered as the water trickled further. She placed the cloth in the water and paused to study her own body. The breasts were firm and small, the waist narrow, the hips a little too wide. The water ran into her pubic hair, it was not an unpleasant sensation. She touched herself down there, fondled the small fuzz of hair with her fingers. Years ago, many years ago, she had been kissed there. She heard a child's cry come from the dormitory. Her self-absorption and self-exploration was over. She seized the wet towel from the bowl, wrung the excess water from it, and rubbed her body hard with rough, cold towelling. She might just as well have been cleaning a car. Her more private regions were now cleaned with the scurrilous contempt that one might give to a dirty window-pane. By the time she was dry the crying from the dormitory had ceased. She climbed into her bed feeling refreshed but ready for sleep. Isobel had learned how to utilise her repression and did not regret that a momentary lapse into sensuality had been smashed by the cry of a child. No one could say that Isobel Quirk was a cold spinster. She was just merely controlled.

'I seem to remember doing this before.' Once more Shirley crawled behind Reuben across the lawn.

The journey was much more simple than the previous one. In fact, Reuben had said that he should make it alone. Shirley had demolished this argument and argued that if anything happened to him the priests would not receive their blankets. The blankets had been parcelled up and strapped to his back in the form of a haversack. Both of them crawled free of hindrance.

'We ought to try for a faster time, a new crawl record,' she quipped.

'Shut up,' he hissed. 'Joking at such times as this is dangerous. Now be quiet.'

They reached the gate and listened for voices. There was no conversation but they could hear the occasional grunt of discomfiture and an intermittent sigh. Then the quiet chanting of prayers began.

'Oh the darlings, Christ help them,' Shirley muttered. She untied the blankets from Reuben's back. 'Blankets, here are blankets for warmth,' she called out.

They tossed the blankets over the wall. The prayers ceased.

'God bless you and your children.' This was the only response they received before the praying recommenced.

'I'll lead the way back, you follow me this time. I know the route, it's good training for me,' said Shirley. As a mark of his trust and as an indication of good faith in her intent

Reuben kissed Shirley's behind. With a double blessing urging her forward, Shirley made no mistakes in course or direction and the couple re-tracked their way back to the house in record time.

Madge gulped at her cup of cocoa as she watched Harry Wintner pull the sheets and blankets from their beds. There was no frantic haste in the way that he went about it. Although, their beds had been pushed together on the previous night (all a question of space) they had been made up separately. Madge had casually remarked that it had got a bit chilly. Harry had agreed with her and promptly observed that they would double the amount of warmth by making the two beds up as one. Madge was too surprised to object but she had said, just as a matter of delicacy, that there was still a crack or small space between them. The sheets now obliterated the crack. He plumped the pillows into place and swiftly had all the blankets neatly in position. He folded back one corner of the bedding and tucked it neatly back under the mattress. This was all achieved in a few minutes; years of expertise in all kinds of domesticity had left their mark upon him. Madge stared at the section of the bedding that was folded back, this opening was the gateway to the night. In spite of her years, Madge felt a little apprehensive.

'You jump in first, old girl. I'll be in a good position to get out in the morning. I can make you a cuppa without waking you up. If you're on the inside it will be easier. We won't be cold tonight.'

Madge held her purple brushed-nylon night-gown firmly round her ankles and climbed into bed. She squirmed and wriggled under the sheets until she had reached the further end of the second bed. Seeking assurance that her position for the night was correct she touched the iron bed-frame with her hand. She watched Harry methodically remove his slippers, switch off the light and she felt only the slightest movement

136

as he slithered into his section of the bed. She spoke after only a few minutes.

'I can't sleep, Harry.'

'What's wrong?' He sounded wounded, worried.

'Oh, nothing personal. I — I — I —' Madge could not finish the sentence and began to whimper. He moved over to her and put his arm about her shoulder. She did not wish to draw away from him. If she had, she would have fallen on the floor. She had begun to cry.

'You've worked yourself into a lather today, you're overwrought,' he snuggled closer to her. His arm moved down to her waist and he hugged her to convey the solace and comfort that he felt for her. She placed her hand on his.

'No, it's not that. It's not that at all. I've forgotten to take my teeth out.'

'Well pass them over, then, I'll put them in the cup for you. No need to upset yourself about that.'

Much to her surprise she extracted them from her jaws and handed them to him. He might just as well have been handling a bouquet of flowers. She heard them plop into the water glass.

He climbed back into bed, she had moved just a little further in from the iron perimeter.

'Now do you want a little cuddle before you drop off?' he asked.

Madge wanted comfort, the feel of his pyjamas were comfortable, his arm about her had felt comfortable, the touch of his hand was reassuring. This was no time for girlish whim or romantic games. She would not lie to him.

'Yes,' she said and turned towards him.

He stroked her a great deal, and patted her head. He kissed her brow, her shrunken lips, and played with the lobes of her ears. She responded gently to him touching him lightly about the head and face. Eventually, he lifted her night-gown and caressed her wrinkled body. She was not driven into ecstasies of passion, no lights exploded in her head as was the fashion in all that she had read about such overtures. Madge was never hypocritical, she let her hand search for him, it found him aroused and wanting her. He entered her gently. She did not gasp with delight but stroked his head.

'At our age we need to share our strength,' he said.

The consummation, unlike that of a young rampant couple, was achieved with the utmost gentleness and tenderness. They whispered to one another, helped one another. When it was over, neither lay back panting with exhaustion, there was no withdrawal, no shared cigarette. Madge saw to it that his pyjama jacket was properly fastened and he adjusted her night-dress. Madge felt relaxed and sleepy.

'You're my sort of woman,' was all he had to say and proved it by encircling her with his arm. In turn, she squeezed his hand.

'Some people might laugh,' thought Madge, 'but so many things were better when you were over sixty. You even appreciated a good morning cup of tea much more.' It was good to be alive and Madge felt alive. If they came through all these troubles she would stay with Harry and ... Both were asleep.

15

Ostanley heard the crash. It came in the early hours of the morning. He usually enjoyed Mondays, but viewing the huge hole in the shattered window of his sitting-room increased his present state of anxiety even further. The house brick had been hurled with great force. The flower-petalled carpet glistened with fragments of broken glass. He winced with pain as a splinter too small for the human eye to see entered and pierced the ball of his foot. He had rushed from his bed on hearing the crash. He glanced at his watch, it was 4.45 a.m. He shrieked at his wife and ordered her back to bed. Bloody stupid idiot, no help at all — only good for one thing. There seemed little point in trying to get any more sleep, he had experienced a fitful night and was glad it was over. It was enough to face his interview at nine o'clock without this happening as well. He felt too frightened to telephone the police, if he did the Guardian Internal Service would be contacted and that would only complicate matters further. He limped into the dining-room, sat at the table and buried his head in his hands; his foot pained him.

He hobbled into the kitchen, perhaps a cup of tea would calm him a little, settle his nerves. Four days ago everything had been going fine, but now everything he did seemed to explode in his face. Even his business seemed to be wavering a little. He had only cleared £2,000 profit from house sales on Friday, and he had spent at least three hours in the office. When all was clear again, he would have a clean sweep at the office, some of the clerks there didn't seem to know what a decent day's work entailed. He picked at his foot. Perhaps his wife had been right about the other matter. Edna had never felt so strongly or entered into the euphoric support that he had chosen to offer the National Conformity Party. She had irritated him by quietly refusing to attend any gatherings or take part in any of their functions. She had even resisted joining the ladies' afternoon-tea group and was adamant about not wishing to stand as a school's guardian.

'I don't like them,' she had said quietly during one break-fast time.

'Don't ever let me hear you talk about the Party like that again, Edna, not in front of me, the children, or anyone else for that matter' he had barked at her.

If she fluttered such opinions around he would never be awarded an order of merit and his business connections would double if he did receive one. Edna was such a goose about such matters, but then most women were. Ostanley disliked women. Edna had been the most passive one he could find; he owned her and treated her as he wished, there was no debate between them. Their children had been born of love-making that resembled a car being filled at a petrol service-station. Edna was required to lie back and wait until the tank was full and then be driven according to his whim and caprice.

He took the card from the shelf. Its simplicity of presentation frightened him:

140

'You are summoned to attend an urgent inquiry with regard to matters pertaining to — school. You are expected at 9 a.m. Monday, June 25th. As State Guardian for this school you will be required to give some account of your actions. What has arisen is of a most serious nature. In this we are invoking a custodial clause to the interview so that if required you could he held here until we deem it fit for you to leave. Should you not attend you will be placed under parochial care and taken into custody immediately. However, we have every faith that you will observe our summons and respond to the call of duty.   R. Lepkiss, Clerk to the GIS'

Edna was the nearest so it was to her he transferred his suffering. He drank his tea and woke up the household by taking a long, noisy bath. He bathed his foot with Dettol and demanded Edna to cook his breakfast at 6.30 a.m. She came down in her housecoat but he sent her back to dress properly.

'I've got a difficult day ahead of me and its not going to help matters if I see my wife staring across the breakfast table at me dressed like a whore.'

She had not replied but silently obeyed him. She was pleased at the opportunity of being able to leave him alone with his boiled eggs. He had decided to arrive at the Guardian Internal Bureau Office early. This would give an indication of his good intent. Edna was required to wave good-bye to him at 8.45 a.m. — the neighbours must not suspect anything. After he had driven away, Edna took a dustpan and brush and swept up the pieces of broken glass. She had been told to say that the window-pane had contracted and shattered because she had mistakenly turned on the central heating instead of the hot water. A pitiful excuse, nevertheless she would obey. She dumped the broken pieces of glass in the dustbin but for some reason she did not remove the house brick from the carpet. She picked it up and examined it carefully. Just an ordinary brick — except that it had sailed through their window. Someone had thrown it at her husband.

She stroked the brick's rough surface and placed it with loving care and respect behind the bookshelves. Souvenirs needed to be treasured.

'There's no doubt about it, you've handled this matter badly. Clumsy would be too kind a word. What you have managed to achieve by your bungling is tantamount to gross negligence of duties. We could charge you for that and make an application for your arrest under Section 89, Guidelines for Conduct of Officers.'

From the moment Ostanley had entered the room the three men sitting round the small table had attacked him with threat after threat. This latest onslaught had come from the large fat man who sat at the centre of the trio. He had never moved from his chair and his declamations were void of any gesticulation of hand or arm. His puffed up face remained without expression, but the jowls of flesh under his chin wobbled as he spoke.

It was the smallest of the three men who gave Ostanley the most serious cause for alarm. When he chose to speak he would leave his seat and encircle Ostanley like a gnat buzzing about in the late summer evening. He was small, almost to the point of being a midget, yet his voice was deep and rasping. Each time he spoke, he leapt from his chair. Ostanley winced, the little man had jumped from his seat once again and was hovering behind Ostanley's left ear. Ostanley wondered whether to turn from the table and face him. His present state of terror left him immobile. In any case, the small man moved about so much it was difficult to face him and be properly attentive to what he had to say. Ostanley was shocked by a sharp pain in the side of his neck. Involuntarily his hand sought to defend the area. The back of his hand received a similar shaft of agony, he leaned sideways and looked back. The small man was holding a needle or a safety-pin.

'Just thought we'd jog a bit of life into you. Acupuncture

for dozy bastards. Get your thinking cap on and do a bit of explaining. Don't cringe, sit up man or you'll get this up your arse, or in your eye. How would you like that?'

Several times he lunged at Ostanley who shielded his neck and face from the searing jabs delivered by the pin. His hands and shoulders received merciless treatment. Ostanley felt sick and dizzy, he began to sway on the chair. His hands could bear no more pain, he could feel the bleeding. He dropped them to his sides.

'Stop. Stop. That's enough Maurice. Sit down.' The fat man grunted his order and the torture ceased. Ostanley broke into hysterical sobs of fear and relief.

'Give yourself time to recover, straighten up now, let's hear what you have to say for yourself. No one wants to hurt you.' The tallest man was the police representative. He spoke sympathetically; his sympathy was part of the attack on the unfortunate man that the trio were interviewing. Frighten them first, then offer friendship, repeat the process if needs be. Eventually they would blab. The police officer genuinely believed Ostanley to be a true idiot, just a bungler who could offer no information. He smiled in Ostanley's direction. Encourage the stupid bastard first and then kick him afterwards. Ostanley had stopped weeping but his frame still shook and his voice quavered.

'I knew nothing of their plans. I had no idea that they had a house at their disposal. I had not been lax in my visiting and had always reported back everything that I knew.'

'There's not a bit of muck here that we can get to work on.'

Maurice waved a sheet of paper in the air. It contained conjectures from Ostanley about relationships within the school. Obviously he had presented the lies in a most unconvincing fashion. Maurice slammed the paper back on the desk.

'The Prentice woman was useless, you invested your time badly there. Was there no one else to work on?' the police representative asked quietly.

Ostanley shook his head. He expected another attack, he broke into another fit of blubbering.

'You can go now.' The fat man's words surprised him.

'I'm free to go?'

The fat man nodded. 'We may need your help at a later date, just call in and register here each morning. That is all we require of you at present. You speak of this matter to no one. Do you hear?'

'Yes sir.' Ostanley answered like a boy scout.

'Off you go then, man. Oh, one more thing. Your hands. You've been pruning rose trees or picking raspberries. Understand?' Maurice allowed a low-pitched giggle.

'You understand?' The fat man repeated the phrase.

'Of course, of course.' Ostanley stumbled from the room and made his way to the lavatory on the second floor. He was forced to discard his underpants before leaving the building.

'Nothing to be going on with here,' the police representative flipped through the files before him. He passed them along to the fat man who patted them with his pudgy hand.

'Any minority groups?' the fat man's mouth moved, his chin wobbled.

'No blacks, nothing from the norm sexually, one Jew, and a Catholic.'

'Political backgrounds — any lapsed activists?'

'Nothing in that line either. They are a boring group. The Jew lived with his mother who is eighty and deaf. The Catholic lived in a hostel for good girls — we've checked the place thoroughly. They'll say nothing about her that we can get our teeth into. Deeply religious and kept herself to herself — lived for her work. No, Miss Bontil and Mr Goldman are asbestos protected. We've gone through all the rest with a nit-comb and come up with nothing.' The police representative spoke apologetically as if to indicate that this was his first big failure at seeking out blame or crime where none was due.

'I could get started with the press. Put it out as a vicious kidnapping operation — perhaps a sexual slant to it?' Maurice tried to cheer up his chief's morose look of indecision. His fat mentor waved a hand in his direction to shut him up.

'Let's hear the worst first,' he turned once more to the officer of police.

'All the parents have posters in their windows stating that their children are in safe care and that they are happy with the situation. This must have been planned beforehand. If the parents have openly passed the wretched kids on, we can hardly push the kidnapping line. In any event, there have been 200 or more people walking around and around the house in Bayswater all day. Three old cranky priests are sitting near the gate and the rest keep walking.'

'Walking?' The fat man lit a cigarette and blew the smoke upwards.

'Yes, they don't say anything. No banners, no placards, they just walk and whisper.'

'Shoot the buggers, demonstrations are against the law.'

'Don't be a fool, Maurice, shut that mouth until you're asked to open it.'

The next puff of smoke was directed at Maurice's head.

'There is nothing to identify the walkers, they don't group. I did hear that the auntie of one of the lads was one of them. I questioned him about her and she's never gone out of the house for the last four years except to a whist drive of a Wednesday. It's difficult to act on something or some people who are so ... so ... what would you say?'

'Unspecific.'

'Yes, chief, you're right. That sums it up.'

'What actions have you taken?'

'The water is cut off, they can't last long without water.'

'No. Extend it to electricity tonight. Telephone gone?'

'Yes.'

'We could go in there as a rescue squad, in defence of the children. We could shoot all the swine then. I could see the press coverage was rightly handled.' Maurice could not keep still or quiet.

'Sit down, keep quiet you fucking pin-head,' the fat man roared at him.

'Do you want martyrs? It's gone too far for that. We must bide time.'

The fat man paused, stroked his chin, and his features spread into a great smile. He proffered a cigarette to the men sitting either side of him.

'Martyrs, martyrs, that's it. We must have a martyr. We'll make one.'

'I don't understand, sir,' said Maurice.

'You wouldn't,' the fat man turned to the police officer. He too looked puzzled. The fat man imprinted his authority, his superb artistry in manipulation and wickedness upon the proceedings.

'Ostanley is our man. When we are ready we will make him a hero. We'll heap rewards on him. Posthumous ones, Listen to my inclinations.' He extolled his plans. Maurice cackled with glee and rubbed his hands together like some manic schizophrenic.

'Brilliant,' murmured the police representative.

'There, there, Tim. Auntie Beryl is here. Timothy, there's a good boy, there's a brave lad. I'm here. You're not on your own. You are with us Timmy. There, there, feeling better now? You are with us. There's a good boy, got a smile for Auntie Beryl, haven't you?'

Beryl wiped the traces of froth and spittle from the mouth of the seven-year-old boy. His eyes which had formerly shot back into the sockets of his skull, unseeing, uncomprehending, now gradually focused themselves upon her. Fits came like lightning, the indications mounted quickly, the dizziness, the pallor seemed to indicate the stormy weather. Beryl had never been afraid of storms. In fact, she rather enjoyed them. Similarly, if a child's seizure was violent she remained calm, did what was required and waited for the attack to break. She liked to think of herself as the epitome of the calm after a storm. Unfortunately, this was the third such storm that the small boy had been forced to weather that day. She felt that it was too much for him. He stroked her face as a nine-month-old child might.

'There, you're back with us again. We are all here.'

She placed him in his bed and was pleased to see him enter a normal sleep. It was his usual pattern. 'I think that we must keep him to his former dosage of pheno-barbs. Isobel asked me to see how he would cope if we decreased it.'

'He's not going to manage without it, poor little soul.' Pauline folded some clean sheets, pulling them into oblong shapes before stacking them carefully away on a higher shelf. She had to stretch in order to push the last sheet in place. Beryl heard the cloth split under the armpit of Pauline's blouse. Pauline looked unusually distressed.

'I haven't had time to iron my other ones yet. This was clean on today.' She placed a hand over the space where the sleeve had departed from the torso of the blouse. 'I can't go about like this. Shirley is using the iron at the moment.'

'Take it off. I can tack it together in ten minutes. Here, put this around you while you are waiting.' Beryl handed Pauline a large bath-towel. Pauline still looked unsure. 'It will cover all of you,' said Beryl.

She set to work and Pauline, to show her appreciation, tried to think up something nice to say.

'You are everybody's auntie, Beryl.'

Beryl reacted badly to this and the cotton snapped. 'Damn, blast.'

'Beryl!' exclaimed Pauline.

'I'm sorry, I thought I'd escaped all of that. It's my own fault.' Beryl re-threaded the needle. 'There, bull's eye first time.'

'I don't understand,' said Pauline referring to Beryl's outburst and ensuing apology.

'I have two brothers, both are married. They run a family butcher shop together. As a child, I was always kept out of the shop. Not encouraged to watch the chopping and labelling

148

of the meat, not encouraged to serve customers. My brothers always apologised to their friends about me whether I was there or not. "Our Beryl is clever" they would say, "but that's as far as it goes." They pointed out very early on that I was not only fat, but plain and it would be useless for me ever to think in terms of marriage. By the time I was nineteen both my parents were dead. Am I boring you, Pauline?'

'No, dear, tell me you'll feel better then. Don't stop sewing though.'

'Well, with both parents dead, I just looked after the domestic side of things for my brothers. You know, cooking, cleaning, washing — that kind of thing. I am two years older than Albert and only eleven months older than Edward. It first started when Edward brought his first girl-friend home. I'd put on a new skirt and a nice jumper and cardigan. I'd got a lovely tea ready. I didn't want to let him down. Albert and Edward must have worked it all out beforehand.'

'What?'

'Edward introduced me to his girl-friend as his Auntie Beryl. Albert called me Auntie throughout the tea. I accepted the role, but it hurt me deeply. I felt very resentful about it. At twenty-four I was designated as an eternal aunt. Capable, kind, practical, someone who was always there and someone who was insufferably dull. My brothers made me feel ugly.'

'That's not true, Beryl, they had no right to —'

'I am plain, I am fat,' said Beryl.

Pauline clutched her towel closer round her shoulders; if only people would look beyond external appearances. Beryl had never declared any kind of suffering before, and here she was telling silly Pauline about her life-long hurts. Pauline felt honoured, she encouraged Beryl to continue.

'The business grew, my brothers absorbed the paper shop next door, they married. Their wives helped in the shops, I was kept on as a domestic. In five years they produced six children between them. There was always a new baby coming and Auntie Beryl became an expert with other people's children. I don't think that my nephews and nieces ever realised it, but they were years of resentment as far as I was concerned. My brothers were appalled when they discovered my intention of going into teacher-training. I had to pay for it myself, I trained as a 'mature student'. After qualifying, I remained at home with them. They never asked about my work, I paid board and lodging and their social friends or even their children's friends all referred to me as Auntie. It was no hardship for me to decide to come here. You see, I feel more related to these children and to you than I did to them. I haven't missed seeing any of them. Is that wicked of me?' Beryl passed the blouse to Pauline. 'Try it now.'

'Fits just as well. No, no, you're not a wicked person. No, no, you are right, we are related,' said Pauline as she buttoned up her blouse.

'You can call me Auntie then, if you want to.'

Both women were laughing as Margaret entered the room with a tray. On the tray were balanced three soup bowls filled with yellow, blue and red liquid. She placed the tray on the floor in the centre of the aisle.

'Aren't they pretty?' she questioned anyone who was about.

Pauline almost always agreed with Margaret. Timothy was asleep, the rest of the children were being looked after by Isobel in the secure play-space outside. This left Beryl open for comment.

'What are they for? We're not doing any painting before bedtime. A story perhaps, but we're not getting them all worked up for painting.' Beryl checked herself and looked at the bowls of coloured water more carefully. Slight dribbles of steam drifted up from the one which was red. Beryl knelt down before the bowls. 'What are they for, Margaret?'

'It was something that I worked out for Timothy. I thought he might enjoy it.'

'He's asleep now, he fitted badly — three times today,' said Pauline.

150

She joined Beryl and knelt beside the bowls.

Such was the spontaneity of Margaret's sense of wonder that quite inadvertently she found herself teaching other teachers to teach. Most paediatricians and almost all teachers would have pronounced Timothy Grace impossible to teach, ineducable, merely a case for care. Margaret was not arrogant but tended to ignore experts if their prognosis was pessimistic. Quadraplegic, brain damaged, prone to severe epilepsy, if left in his cot he would whimper and shudder in between the times that the epilepsy had not seized control of him. However, he had learned to smile, he had learned to accept and reject. Ostanley, on first viewing him, had said that he was a cabbage, a cabbage. Cabbages could do none of the things that Timothy could do with more meaning than most adults. Margaret sought to extend him further. She joined the other two women on the floor and sat back on her heels. None of her postures looked uncomfortable for her, but anyone trying to emulate her positions might have found themselves in an extreme state of agony or with a slipped disc.

'Now, girls, dip when I tell you to.' Pauline looked bewildered at Margaret's suggestion. 'Just place your forefinger in the bowl when I call out the colour.' Margaret anticipated the results of the experiment with all the relish of a scientist who was about to view the culmination of a decade of research. 'Blue,' she called. 'How does it feel, girls?'

'Cold,' Beryl flatly replied. Pauline agreed with her. 'Red.'

'It's hot, almost too hot,' Pauline added withdrawing her finger hastily.

'Yellow.'

'Warm, it's warm.' Beryl was beginning to sense some enlightenment as to the meaning of the bowls. 'You don't think that we can teach Timothy his colours by dipping about like this do you?' she asked.

'I don't know, I really don't know, but would you say that sensations are important?'

'Oh yes,' said Pauline who was more afraid of her own sense of touch than most people.

'Well if we can help him to discriminate between cold, warm and hot, might he not only discern, but enjoy. Close your eyes.'

The two pupils did as they were bid. Margaret dipped their fingers into the bowls and called out the appropriate sensation. Beryl accepted the usefulness of the exercise and Pauline was, as usual, entranced by yet another of Margaret's activities. The two women opened their eyes to see Leslie Murt viewing the operation. He had chosen not to interrupt it.

'I come to tell you that Isobel wishes to call a staff-meeting after the evening meal tonight. Apparently she has matters to discuss and a few others are anxious to bring up other proposals.'

'What other proposals?' She let go of Pauline's forefinger which dropped into the hot bowl and spilled some of its contents on the floor.

'I don't know,' said Leslie. He spoke truthfully.

'What are you up to now?' he asked.

'Testing,' said Margaret.

'What?' he asked.

'Oh, sensations. I think that what we feel is very important, don't you?'

'Oh yes, very important — couldn't agree more,' he called over his shoulder as he left the room.

He found Isobel in the playground, she had the children sitting about her doing individual activities. Isobel was a great believer in the importance of solitary forms of play. Whereas Margaret taught adventurously, intuitively almost, Isobel, who was not blest with Margaret's inherent imagination, had to plan to the last detail in order to be successful. The special-care children had always been the biggest challenge for her. A plan could quickly dissolve, instantly fail and it was often necessary to resurrect interest quickly, instantly. Isobel could only achieve this by having a number of planned activities stored up in her mind. She rarely experienced a flash of sudden insight that led to an inspired lesson. However, she was an acute observer and her eventual success with the children lay in her capacity for utilising her observations to their best advantage. Isobel Quirk was not a 'natural' teacher, part of her success lay in the fact that she had little real histrionic ability to fall back on, therefore, she had no choice but that of attempting to learn something from her pupils every day. She was never mean about the skills which she had painstakingly acquired, she shared these skills with her staff in as modest a fashion as was possible and presented them to the children with as much verve and éclat as she could muster.

Leslie picked up a sad-looking child who had begun to grizzle and cry. The child could not be exhorted or cajoled into being interested in the assorted shapes and sizes of the coloured wooden blocks that had been set before him.

'I was hoping he would share what he was doing with Jane, she's happy and interested enough but there is no fascination nor meaning in it for him. I'm afraid he's feeling a bit disgruntled. Perhaps I'll try him on something else.'

Isobel always maintained more formality with Leslie than any other member of her staff. This distancing from her deputy was as carefully planned and maintained as the activities that she had set before the children. As with the children, her resources were not always successful with him. On such occasions when they failed, she lapsed into a routine and ritual of expression which Leslie had come to dislike. He felt sorry for her when she had to deploy such defence mechanisms; being a tolerant man he had never pointed them out to her. Nothing on earth could give Leslie the impetus to cause Isobel the slightest hurt, even if it was for her own good. Such was the extent and depth of his love for her.

'I've let them all know about the staff meeting. After

dinner tonight, somewhere between 7.30 and 8.00 p.m. Is that all right?'

He offered the squawking child on his knee a wooden brick. The child would not be comforted and flung it from him and continued to cry louder than before. Leslie had to raise his voice to make himself properly heard.

'Does that time suit you?' he bawled.

Isobel took the child from him and began to interest him in a pocket kaleidoscope.

'Yes, it's fine,' she said. The whimpering and crying stopped. She glanced at her watch. 'Yes, that couldn't be better, I'll get the children upstairs now.'

'Let me give you a hand.' She accepted his offer of help without comment, she sensed that he had more to say. Leslie often delivered the most important piece of information or insights when he was not in direct discussion, it was though his large hands hindered his mind and brain. If his hands were occupied he managed to essay the most important things as though they were asides. Isobel always paid close attention to Leslie's asides. He began gathering the wooden blocks together making sure to place them in perfect symmetry in the adjacent tray. Isobel was busy marshalling the children who were not mobile together in one group. He looked in Isobel's direction.

'Leave me to carry them upstairs, I can manage two at a time. It will only need a couple of journeys.'

She nodded her thanks. He lifted one child and she passed him another. He grasped them firmly, one under each arm. The human package gurgled with delight as he spun them round.

'I think you should expect trouble,' he panted.

'Why?'

'There have been other meetings, something's going on, I don't like it.'

'I can't be worried about people's private discussions, Leslie.' She answered his warning with prim formality.

'I'll worry for you, then; only be prepared for something. I don't know what, if I did I would tell you.'

'We'd better get the children upstairs,' she said.

A ripple of goose-pimples spread along her arms and across the back of her neck. She was not afraid of the outside forces working against her — but she had not contemplated serious trouble from within. Leslie was no scaremonger. What could there be to worry about? Which of her helpers were dissatisfied, unhappy? What had she done wrong? Had she upset anyone? Isobel had no time to give the matter any further thought. She finished marshalling the children together and began to lead them upstairs. The goose-pimples on her arms remained. Fortunately, Leslie had no way of observing Isobel's manifestation of her fear. Like many people, the unknown made her feel uncomfortable. However, unlike most people she was not fortunate enough to be in a position where she could express her fears.

'You won't forget the other two children will you, Leslie?' She called up to him as he climbed the stairs ahead of her.

'You're not worried?' he called back.

'No,' Isobel lied. There was no sense in sharing her anguish when it could be contained, or could it be that she was afraid to appear to be too vulnerable? That wouldn't be a good thing. She hugged the child nearest to her, this was as much consolation as she would allow herself.

More work was involved in the preparation and cooking of the evening meal than either Harry or Madge had anticipated. It was odd how you could take something like a water tap for granted. Madge had muttered something similar to this to Harry when their watches indicated to them that the meal would be on the table almost an hour and a half later than had been arranged. Madge had almost become tearful over the rice which had absorbed more water than she had given it credit for; she whimpered as she dug the wooden spoon into the burned granules at the bottom of the saucepan.

'Don't worry, the curry will take the burnt edge off it.'

Margaret had comforted her. In different circumstances Madge might have felt a little jealous of Margaret; a real daughter could easily have felt some resentment about the special turn in her relationship with Harry. Margaret had probably not yet assessed the depth of their relationship, but she had an odd manner of accepting everything; to Margaret nothing ever seemed out of the ordinary. Madge had always liked her — such colourful clothes. Margaret had trained Harry's mongol child well, a dear, loving girl who was helpful and not at all demanding. It was quite clear that Margaret adored her foster-father and his child; Madge discarded any fears that lurked in her head; at her age it was of no use being possessive about the past. The past details of Harry's life must not impinge on her present view of him. Therefore, the less she knew about it the better. If he chose to tell her, then she would listen. She scooped the mountain of boiled rice into the enamel tureen.

'Dinner is being served, dinner, ladies and gents. Dinner is being served.'

She bawled through the house as she carried the steaming bowl into the dining-room.

It was dark outside by the time it was convenient for the staff meeting to commence. The washing of the main dishes had been completed and a new austerity had dispensed with an evening cup of tea or cocoa. People had nothing to sip. Shirley sat in a large chair with her legs curled beneath her. For some reason she had chosen not to bring her knitting along. She entwined her fingers together as if in idleness they might wander away from her. Margaret was busy putting different coloured darns on a pullover which was full of holes. It wasn't necessary for Isobel to call the meeting to order, there was little or no movement and no chatter.

'If everyone is ready I would like to open the meeting. I

know that some of you are very tired. As we do not have an agenda, I have prepared a report on our situation so far, it might be helpful if you would make your comments known afterwards. May I begin?'

Isobel had stood in readiness to make her report.

'I'd like to make a point of order first,' Shirley spoke quickly, quietly.

Margaret placed her darning on the floor, a patch incomplete. Suddenly, the meeting had become more alert. Isobel sat down and waited.

'Let's have the report first and the points of order afterwards,' Leslie made his contribution without trying to hide the grumpy tone in his voice.

'I would prefer that, if it is all right with you, Shirley?' Isobel was extremely polite. Shirley unclenched her hands and made only the slightest gesture.

'Carry on, I'll make it later.'

Isobel stood once more.

'So far everything has gone as well as we could have hoped for. First, let me say how very much I appreciate the hard work and effort that you have all put into this undertaking.'

Isobel's voice wavered, she was conscious of the fact that she sounded as though she were making an oration about an end of term school project or a Christmas play. She felt the need for more emotion, less objectivity, her feelings told her this but her long training in educational spheres lacerated her exposition of these feelings. She wanted to cry before them, declare tears of gratitude, ask for their love, plead for an acceptance of her inadequacies, state all her misgivings, discuss their individual aims and indeed what might be their destinies. Instead she cleared her throat and approached the report as though she were making out an inventory for a furnished flat.

'The children do not seem to be suffering from their change of environment and have adjusted well to their new surroundings. Pauline and Beryl have borne the brunt of the hard work involved in such a metamorphosis and I know that you will all agree with me in proffering congratulations.'

Assent was murmured by everyone and Isobel plodded on to the next item.

'I thought it better to stick to the more pastoral sides of this operation first and I did say that as in a school, some of our duties would be quite defined and that some of them would overlap and blur. At certain times the pressure is more intense in one area than in another. However, it seems to me that Madge and Harry have a particularly insistent burden catering and cooking for all our needs.'

As if to prove Isobel's point, Madge had nodded off into quite a heavy sleep. Any pauses that Isobel made were filled with gentle snoring noises and heavy breathing from Madge's chair. Harry sat next to Madge and occasionally checked to see if she was comfortable and that her teeth stayed in place. No one chose to wake her.

'I suggest that a rota be formulated involving myself, Margaret, Leslie, Reuben and Shirley to help with things like clearing dishes and washing up — that is, if we are not otherwise engaged in some kind of imperative activity.'

'I don't think anyone will want to quibble about helping Madge and Harry,' said Leslie.

The others nodded their heads in agreement. Isobel felt better now, she cleared her throat.

'I'd like to make my point of order now.' Shirley spoke in restrained cool fashion. Leslie once more began to protest. Isobel sat down.

'Make your point, Shirley, it seems urgent to you. Please make it now.'

Isobel did not wish to shelter under Leslie's gruff defence any longer. It was strange how both she and Leslie sensed an attack. Isobel waited for the onslaught from within.

'It's about the position of chairman, chairperson.' Shirley corrected herself.

'We've settled that position,' Leslie interjected.

158

'I don't agree that we have, at least, we have not settled it democratically. You must realise, Isobel, that there is nothing personal in what I am about to say.'

Shirley only half-glanced in Isobel's direction, nevertheless Isobel answered her.

'I'm sure there isn't, Shirley. Don't feel restrained.'

'Isobel was appointed as head teacher of a school. It's true that all but one of the staff of that school are here with her now. However, none of us are bound by the rules of the authority that appointed her. Indeed, we have flouted those rules and broken laws. Our presence here, now verifies this point. If you wish to give us a broad title we are part of an action committee which has been set up in defiance of the State. We are not embalmed in a cosy building from nine until five. We are committed to a cause which alienates us from what could be loosely termed as the protection of the State. In discarding that protection, in defying it we are ... whether you like the term or not ... we are revolutionaries.'

'I hadn't thought of it like that,' said Pauline.

'No, that's the point I am making, we must think, think more deeply about the strengths and weaknesses of our corporate position. Our individual reasons for being here should not count for so much. That is why I am proposing a different chairman for the period of time that we are here, for the time that we are in the state of siege. That time has already begun.'

Shirley had not stood to make her contribution, but did so when she had finished speaking. Isobel admired her skill, Shirley had controlled her bad temper and presented her case well.

'I'm not having any part in this, Isobel is our chairman. We should not allow another vote.'

Isobel noted the hurt and injury in Leslie's voice, for him there could be no revolution unless he was allowed this subservience to her, no other voice joined his protest and Isobel waited for a little more response. The silence bit into her, clearly she did not have unqualified support. It was up to her

159

to defend her position, to direct Shirley's argument. Could she revert back to the needs of the children? No, she would not use them. She waited and listened to Madge who had now lapsed into heavy snoring. Isobel was glad that the dear old scout had been spared the tension. Margaret broke it.

'I think we should vote.' She picked up her patches and began to sew one on the elbow of a pullover.

'No, no, don't, if we vote —'

'You wish to nominate someone else as chairman?' Isobel's question cut Leslie short. Isobel hated to silence him, but took her lead from Margaret.

'I nominate Reuben,' said Shirley.

'I second that,' said Beryl.

Isobel caught her breath, this was a surprise.

'I nominate Isobel,' Margaret sucked a piece of cotton before pushing it through the eye of the needle first time. She appeared unconcerned with the nature of the proceedings.

'Seconded,' boomed Leslie.

'Let's have a show of hands. It's the quickest.'

Margaret's contribution remained flippant. She had always been a good actress. Isobel felt a sense of relief when only two hands were raised in favour of Reuben.

'Two votes for Reuben.' Shirley seemed intent on stating the obvious.

Leslie, Margaret and Pauline voted for Isobel. Hands were lowered. Isobel looked in Shirley's direction. It had been Shirley's motion, let her state the conclusion.

'Isobel is chairperson — carried by three votes to two with two abstentions.'

'Is that it, then?' asked Margaret.

'Of course,' said Shirley. Reuben remained impassive seemingly neither pleased, nor displeased at the outcome. Madge had slept through it all and Harry had chosen to align himself with no one. He had never voted in his life, nor was he tempted to now.

160

'Leslie, I wonder if you could give us a report on the extent of communication that we have made?' Isobel proceeded with the meeting as formerly planned.

'The response has been better than expected; although the authorities are aware of us, they have hit back cautiously. The telephone is dead, and water has been cut off. We are coping. All day up to 200 or 300 people have been walking around the house. They are not being obstructive, just walking and talking. Three priests seem to be permanently ensconced in the gateway. I believe that these people are supporting us in the only way that they know how.' He glanced out of the window. 'Many of them are still there, it's as though they were watching over us.'

'Bearing witness,' Pauline added.

'I'd like to go out and meet some of them, just to talk to them and thank them, after all they don't know us,' Margaret mused, wistfully rather than hopefully.

'It's not at all practical, I should know that. Try crossing that lawn and you're done for,' said Shirley.

'I agree with you, Shirley,' said Isobel. 'It is not a practical proposition but I don't think that Margaret was suggesting it as such.'

'No, I wasn't,' Margaret involuntarily shuddered at the thought of the lawn impregnated with destruction. Whereas the idea of it thrilled Shirley, it appalled Margaret.

'This brings us directly on to our modes of defence. In effect, we have already been attacked. As Leslie has stated, the telephone is dead and the water has been cut off. We have to manage without the telephone and as far as Reuben can assess, we have limitless supplies of water here within the building.' Isobel waited a moment, Madge had awoken with a snort and was anxious to pretend that she had not been asleep. Harry patted her arm. 'Even so, there is a need to use the water sparingly, only children are allowed baths and this must be restricted to a twice weekly routine. The heating and delivering of the water is arduous — but no more so than it was for the people who first lived in this house.'

'Yes, the Victorians managed, so why can't we?' Beryl enjoyed the prospect of being transported back in time.

Isobel continued. 'Should the gas be affected we have Calor supplies for two and a half months, as yet it has not been tampered with. It seems to be a process of smoking us out gently. It is clear they want us out, but they are uncertain as to what methods to use. I think that we are an embarassment to them and that they would like us extradited from here with as little bother and fuss as possible.'

'They won't manage that, no, never. There's the embryo of a bother just outside the gates now and it will grow. It must grow,' said Shirley.

'We can only hope for more support, if —'

The room and the whole house were plunged into complete and sudden darkness.

For a few moments no one spoke. A sigh of dismay rose from the crowd of people that encircled the house.

'Give them light,' someone bawled into the night air.

'A supporter,' said Beryl.

'They have cut off the electricity.' Reuben spoke gently but his manner of speaking indicated to Isobel that she was expected to make a decision. There was no time to plan, she must trust her emotions, her instinct.

'Light the paraffin lamps. Hold one to every window, let them see that we are blazing with light. We will ration later. But for now, light the lamps everywhere. Let them see we have light.'

The house beamed from every window. A cheer rose from the crowd outside. A victory no matter how short, demanded some rejoicing.

17

The beginning of September was not gentle as sometimes that particular month proves to be. It was colder than was usual for the time of the year and there was more rain to accompany it. The elements proved irascible and unkind. On the third day of the month, Brother James coughed and wheezed and gulped. What air his lungs could cope with he absorbed through sharp intakes of breath through his open mouth. Sympathisers had erected a tarpaulin cover over the three old men, but this afforded scant shelter from the damp and cold. A number of people had gathered outside the entrance to witness or to stare at what was happening within. It held more fascination than a road accident; no ambulance was going to arrive to curtail the excitement of pending death. Brother James's eyes became glazed and a hoarse rattling noise came from his throat; his body shook. The other two brothers remained diligently at his side. The rattling ceased quite suddenly, was followed by a short convulsion and then he lay quite still. Father Thomas closed the eyelids and Brother Matthew straightened the legs.

'It's all over, we've all got to go sometime.' Miriam turned to her friend Ruby who had begun to cry. 'I'd grown quite fond of them.' she added.

'He's entitled to a church burial, I'll see that he has it. He is, isn't he?'

Father Thomas raised his head and felt it necessary to break his vow of silence.

'Yes, madam, he is. I will give you an address. I will be grateful if you make such an arrangement. We cannot leave this spot. You understand?'

'Of course, don't you worry. Leave it to us,' said Ruby, who was greatly moved.

'God be with you,' was all Father Thomas said, and Ruby and Miriam wasted no time in going about their sad but urgent business.

Pressures were brought upon the hierarchial establishment of the church to remove the body as quietly as possible. The establishment within the church tacitly agreed, after all burials were always quiet, always solemn, nevertheless certain high ranking individuals made it quite plain that Brother James would be mentioned at the Sunday service. His death swelled the crowds outside the house; there was little weeping, certainly no overt or noisy reactions. But as one of the elderly policemen observed, 'A silent, thinking crowd is the worst to handle.'

The tarpaulin cover had become a Mecca for thinking Christians and there seemed to be more of these around than the State had envisaged. If they weren't all Christians, and they probably weren't, then only God knew the myriad of motives which deemed their presence there. Some of them even questioned His infallibility, but this did not dampen their respect for an old man who had chosen to spend his life and death in prayer for others. In the present state of things, this was tantamount to disobedience; caring should not be spontaneous but directed. At the highest levels, the government were most concerned with this demonstration of blatant individuality.

'We move tomorrow. Eleven in the morning is the deadline. I want them all out. I want them out, the lot of them and I want them alive.' The fat man viewed his subordinates, he used the butt-end of one cigarette to light another. He stubbed the finished cigarette into an ash-tray already brimming with debris. A piece of cellophane caught alight and a small flame burst from the contents of the tray. He glanced at it and watched it burn itself out, ignoring the trail of smoke that drifted into the air. He turned to his police representative.

'What numbers are you making the force?'

'I thought somewhere in the region of between 4 and 500.'

'Too many, make it 250 men at the most. Has Ostanley been contacted?'

'Yes.'

'Keep him in custody here overnight. See that he is comfortable.' He turned to the small man sitting at his side. 'Are all your arrangements complete, Maurice? I want a hero. Have you got him prepared?'

Maurice prodded the ash-tray, it ceased to smoke.

'There will be press releases in all the evening papers, coverage on radio and television. We have photographs of him with his wife and children. Stalwart citizen, family man, pillar of the community, he'll be a saint within two hours of dying.'

The fat man lifted his left thigh from his seat and farted. 'Right then; we'll stink the buggers out tomorrow.' His body shook as he laughed. The others took this as a cue for relaxation and duly joined him in his mirth. The odour around the table was distinctly bad, but no one opened a window to let in some fresh air; they laughed loud and breathed deeply.

Leslie Murt lowered his binoculars and passed them to Isobel who stood at his side. The attic window was open.

'Don't touch the centre piece, they're in focus. You have a clear view, just hold them to your eyes.'

'How many people would you say were there?' Isobel could see the crowds walking about and around the outside walls of the house. None carried placards; apart from the two priests near the gate entrance all were mobile. They kept moving but did not go far from the wall. Fifteen or so policemen kept a watch on the proceedings. If anyone did stop walking they were asked to move along. Any groups which formulated were quickly dispersed.

'I should say there are about 500 people. It varies, I recognise some, they have been around for weeks. The numbers have grown. We get more in the early evening. I think people drop in for a walk round on their way home from work. Some take the day off I suppose. I don't know how long they will keep it up.'

Isobel returned the binoculars to him. 'For as long as we are here, for as long as we can last out,' she rested her head on his shoulder. 'We can't last much longer, can we Leslie?' she gazed out of the open window.

'No, my dear, I don't think we can. What did you expect?'

'I always expected eventual defeat; it is the manner of that defeat which will discern our actions. I must take another look at Timothy, he is still in a coma, I don't think he'll come out of this fit alive.'

'Wasn't that his medical prognosis?'

'Oh, yes, he's gone over the time allocated to him by nearly three years.'

'I'll join you.'

Isobel found Pauline crying. Beryl sat on a chair and stared blankly in front of her as though she had been deafened, struck dumb and blinded simultaneously. Margaret was binding a bandage about the child's head and jaw. She wiped some spittle from his mouth.

166

'It's all over. He's gone,' she said. She wrapped his body in a sheet and pinned it about him to form a shroud.

'I'll take him,' said Leslie. He lifted the inert child in his arms. Margaret followed him out of the room. Death did not shock her. She turned to the other three women, but directed her words more towards Beryl who was in most need of them.

'He knew his colours; he knew three of his colours, didn't he?'

Beryl nodded and Pauline collected her grief. It wouldn't be a good thing for the rest of the children to see them downcast. Margaret had been quite right; Timothy had learned some colours and had often smiled. Quite a lot really. He wasn't a child one could easily forget. Certainly, he had made the most of what fragment of life had been thrown his way and he'd returned the investment to the people who surrounded him. None of the household failed to mourn his death, in this they were well qualified, as all of them had valued his life.

The child was buried a few yards from the house. Leslie had removed a small rose-bush in order to dig the pit deep. He replanted the rose-bush on top of the mound of earth.

'It's the wrong time of the year for transplanting. I don't think that the roots will take.' Harry Wintner made his observation as Leslie patted the earth around the shrub with the spade.

'The rain will help, it will flower next year.'

Margaret had not bothered to cover her head, the others stood about with coats clutched over their heads and shoulders. At a slight signal from Isobel they returned indoors. Isobel joined Leslie who was removing soil and clay from the insteps of his boots.

'There, I don't want to trundle all this mess into the house.'

She watched him remove the last traces of mud with a piece of tissue paper. His boots were quite clean, but he continued wiping away at the soles. He did not look up as she spoke.

'I'll tell them tomorrow night,' she said.

He grunted an assent, stopped wiping his shoes and faced her.

'You've made a decision?'

Isobel nodded. Then she surprised him.

'Would you mind just holding me for a moment? That's all, just hold me for a moment would you?'

'My hands are caked with dirt....' He held her to him.

'We must try to strike a bargain with the authorities, if they guarantee the lives of the children, we will leave peacefully.'

'Their guarantee would be worthless, you know that.'

'If we insisted that the parents would be there to receive them at the gates, there would be witnesses. It's a crude ploy, but it is all that I can think of. I am exhausted, Leslie. We're all exhausted. Madge is ill, her leg is badly ulcerated. She had been keeping it a secret. Harry told me that it needs urgent medical attention, she needs a doctor. The children are looking pale. I cannot face another death, or accept a death in this situation. I think the majority of the adults here will agree with me.'

'I think they will,' he said.

She sighed and eased herself away from his arms. 'Is there any point in thinking about what they will do with us when we leave here? I suppose we will be separated, that will be the hardest part. Leslie, it's my birthday today. I am forty-two years old.'

'You don't look it,' he added quickly.

'And next year, next year....'

'You will be forty-three, we can all count,' he said. He did not offer birthday congratulations, he knew that Isobel was contemplating the last year of her life. Who was he to rupture such private contemplation? It would seem that he ought to be thinking about himself in such a way; try as he might, he could not. If Isobel were around then, and only then, did he feel relevant. After she was gone, then he might try to put some mental pieces together. Leslie was not a philosopher. He followed her into the house.

The loudspeaker shocked everyone in the house. It blared forth quite suddenly. After the initial shock, the inmates gathered in the downstairs sitting-room. Isobel opened the French windows. The prepared message blasted itself into the room. It was repeated at ten-second intervals. Some of the children began to whimper. The voice echoed insistently.

'We want a peaceful outcome. We want you to think of the children in your care and not of yourselves. Please assemble yourselves in the main concrete courtyard of the house. We will make no attempt to cross the lawns.'

'They'd be bloody sorry if they did. The bastards,' Shirley muttered.

'Do we have a hand speaker?' Isobel almost whispered.

'We have a hand-grenade,' Shirley hissed.

Reuben restrained her from rushing downstairs.

'Don't be hasty, think of the children,' he commanded.

170

Shirley remained at his side, clutching his small waist with her hand. Leslie moved slowly, as though he were involved in some afterthought which required some slender activity.

'I'll get the hand speaker for you.'

'Bring it down to the courtyard, we will all be there.'

Isobel waited for the inevitable disagreements but none came. Shirley left Reuben's side and approached Isobel. She took her hand.

'Madam Chairperson, may I be allowed to take just two grenades? I promise not to endanger the lives of the children or anyone else.'

'In that case, you will have no need of the grenades,' said Isobel.

'They're for myself; one is for me and one is for Reuben. We have talked about it together, neither of us can face the prospect of captivity.'

Isobel questioned Reuben with her eyes.

'Oh, no, Shirley. No Reuben,' Margaret cried.

'We would be grateful if you would accept our joint cowardice, we need the grenades. It is an individual choice.' Reuben appealed to Isobel.

'I love him,' said Shirley.

'It will only affect us two. Surely you understand?' Reuben's usually restrained modulation of tone broke as he looked towards Isobel. He opened his arms as though he were appealing to a great multitude. Isobel nodded.

'Yes, I understand. Take them, use them only as you have promised.'

Isobel felt Shirley's dry lips brush her cheek.

'You don't know what will happen to the rest of us?' Pauline picked up a child and held it closely to her. Isobel shook her head. The voice from the loudspeaker reverberated through the room.

'We had best make our way to the courtyard. Harry would you help Madge? The rest of us can manage the children.'

Isobel and Margaret led the way and three or four minutes

later the strange contingent had assembled itself outside on the concrete.

All the children were sat against the wall of the house. Beryl and Pauline sat with them singing rhymes and playing pat-a-cake. Madge leaned on Harry's shoulder and offered to hold his child for him. He refused and stood against the wall, one arm around his child and one about his ill and ageing lover.

Reuben and Leslie stood 10 yards further on at the edge of the concrete. There had been no plan evolved as to these positions, the adults had slotted in where they would choose. The other three women stood right against the edge of the lawn. Isobel had positioned herself there first, Margaret and Shirley had followed, so that now the three of them stood together at the forefront of the company, some 15 yards ahead of the men. Isobel raised the hand speaker to her mouth.

'Let us speak to the parents of the children in our care.' Her voice, which was not loud in any circumstances, came out in a shriek as her vocal chords took the strain. The babble of voices from outside the wall seemed to wither. All that could be heard were the thin, shrill voices of Beryl and Pauline who continued to sing. Isobel received no verbal answer. The women watched one helmet appear, then another, and another. The armed police sat astride the wall, their black rain-capes falling from their shoulders. Once in position, they remained still.

'Clay pigeons,' Shirley murmured.

'I think they look like crows, black crows. Or is it rooks that sit like that?' Margaret asked.

'Let us speak to the parents.' Isobel shrieked into the speaker. More policemen bobbed up into position and sat astride the wall. A group of four or five policemen and four men in civilian clothes pushed open the gate. the hinges had been removed, and the group seemed to be in some kind of agitated discourse on the edge of the lawn. One of the civilians was thrown to the ground and all three women witnessed the kicking. He was hauled on his feet again as though he were a glove puppet.

'It's Mr Ostanley. They've been kicking Mr Ostanley.' Margaret uttered her words with a mixture of horror and surprise.

'I think that this looks bloody nasty.'

Ostanley was given a heavy blow in the solar plexus as Shirley spoke. Then one of the men seized him by the hair and hurled him onto the lawn.

'Oh, dear God, they are making him cross the lawn.' Isobel began to sweat with the realisation. She shrieked into the speaker

'The lawn is detonated. You'll kill him. Don't make him cross the lawn. You'll kill him, you'll kill him.'

Ostanley knelt on all fours, afraid to stand, afraid to sit; he shook his head from side to side like some demented rabid spaniel. Something was shouted to him, the women could not discern the words, the black rooks remained silent and still perched across the walls. Ostanley rose slowly and stood scarecrow-like on the lawn. An object, probably a stone, was thrown from one of the civilians. Ostanley's head jerked backwards in pain as it struck him in the middle of the back. He staggered forwards.

'No, no, no,' Isobel screamed into the speaker.

Ostanley paused and wavered, he swayed to and fro. Another stone struck his leg, he winced at this final impetus, and began most deliberately to limp across the lawn. Isobel threw the speaker to the ground and ran towards him shouting as she ran. Shrieking, ordering him to stop. Margaret and Shirley were at her side and all three ran with their arms raised and their voices pitched high and shrill in warning.

The deafening crash of the explosion caused most of the onlookers to cover their heads or shield their eyes with their forearms. Harry, Leslie and Reuben sought no such cover. They watched the three bodies twist, arch and turn in the air as the blast hit them. No one moved, the smoke cleared. Ostanley appeared to be shielding his eyes. For the moment, he might have welcomed his consequent blindness. Strewn across the lawn were the broken, inert and lifeless bodies of the three women.

'Follow me, the lawn is quite safe now.'

It was Reuben who spoke first. The others obeyed him carrying the children in their arms, not looking to the left or the right. Not glancing at the policemen who maintained their vigil from the wall. Some of the crowd from outside had pushed their way into the entrance of the gate. They watched Beryl take the blinded Ostanley and lead him towards them. They watched with peculiar intent the great care that was taken in leading out the whimpering children. Much to her own astonishment, Pauline was not afraid. One of the group of civilian bullies grabbed her arm and tried to take away the child she held. She spat at him and pulled back.

'Don't move. Any of you.'

Reuben raised the hand-grenades. One in each hand, his forefingers ready to release the pins. The policemen and the Internal Government official stepped back. Two old priests and two women broke through and the crowd and approached Reuben. He still held his hands aloft, the grenades ready. Leslie stood near his left side and Madge had squatted on the floor immediately to his left. One of the women spoke to Pauline.

'Pass the children on to us, dear, we want them to live darlin', we've been here every day. We have, haven't we Ruby?' she turned to her friend for support.

'Yes, dear, so have these lovely gentlemen. They've not moved from the gate. Not since you've been here, they haven't. There were three but one passed over yesterday. Yes, Miriam and me have bought food for them every day. We are here on account of the children. There are lots out there will look after them, we know them. They've talked about nothing else for days — pass the children out to us.'

Pauline looked to Reuben and Leslie for some enlightenment as to how she should respond. Both men nodded their heads. Pauline handed the child to the old priest. He blessed the child and handed it over to Miriam. She scuttled with the child in her arms and passed it into the crowd. Pauline watched the small boy disappear at the end of this human chain.

'The others, be quick, pass the others. We have it organised.'

Beryl obeyed Ruby and thrust a child into her arms. Miriam returned for another. Reuben stood and watched the proceedings, arms held aloft. The Internal Guardians in civilian clothes began to talk. A fat man seemed to be busy giving orders. Harry, Madge and Leslie sensed that they must act quickly. They took up the remaining children in their arms and hurrying with them passed them into the outstretched arms of the waiting crowd.

A wave of cheering broke from the crowd, sections began rhythmic clapping and chants of support. The policemen lining the walls and pavements lowered their guns. Reuben turned back into the entrance of the grounds of the house. His colleagues followed him across the lawn to where the three bodies lay. All of the corpses were badly shattered so that it was impossible to distinguish one woman from another. Only the fragments of clothing gave any clue as to identification. The strange group sat at the edge of the crater. Reuben placed the grenades on the ground. One of the policemen sitting on the wall shouted something, then threw his gun to the ground and disappeared from the wall. Another one quickly followed his example, a huge roar of approval came from the crowd. One by one the helmets and black capes left their positions.

'Get them back, I'll have the buggers shot,' the fat man cried. The police superintendent shook his head, he sensed a change, it had been coming for some time and who was to know who would be in power next. At this rate people might want to vote again, he did not want to be too heavily associated with the present regime. He waved his arm, giving the signal for the rest of his men to disperse. The gesture was largely obsolete as many of them had already begun to walk away, some were chatting to people within the crowd. He turned to the fat man.

'I'll report to you tomorrow. You wouldn't think a bunch of crippled kids could have managed all this.'

The fat man did not answer him, he was aware that the present Government of National Uniformity had been bitten, eaten, its eventual decline was inevitable; his stomach churned. Fear always gave him dyspepsia.

Four hours later the three bodies were removed from the lawn. There were no arrests and nothing was reported by the media. The fragments of cloth and blood remained on the lawn for some time, until eventually all traces were washed away by the winter rain. No history of them was recorded but their credibility bore fruit at the election which was forced upon the country in the following summer.

I'm looking over, a four leafed clover
That I overlooked before.
Some times it's sunshine, and sometimes it's rain
Sometimes it's....